Bad Mood at Cheerful

As if deep in thought, Levi moved so that his hand was closer to the butt of his .45. Even as he did a voice in the back of his mind spelled out the reality of his situation. He knew he could normally draw and shoot before a man could squeeze the trigger. He also knew that however much Myra had worked with his hands, they were still stiff from his fight with Ike.

Not only that, with this man's finger tight against the trigger, his reflexes would squeeze off at least one round even after he was shot. And then both men would die.

Levi Hill had been in some tight situations before. This time he could see no way out, until a last-ditch, desperate idea flashed in his mind. If it worked he might just survive to identify the killer who had already claimed so many victims. Now, Levi's life was truly on the line.

Bad Mood at Cheerful

Billy Hall

A Black Horse Western

ROBERT HALE · LONDON

ISBN 0 7090 7787 4

Robert Hale Limited
Clerkenwell House
Clerkenwell Green
London EC1R 0HT

Typeset by
Derek Doyle & Associates, Shaw Heath.
Printed and bound in Great Britain by
Antony Rowe Limited, Wiltshire.

CHAPTER 1

Cheerful.

He chuckled quietly at the crude sign.

CHEERFUL
Wyoming Territory
Welcome

'Good name for a town. Wonder if it is. Wonder if the welcome's gonna be better'n what we usually get.'

The dog that panted beside his horse appeared to take no notice. The rider pushed his hat up from his forehead, letting it rest on the back of his head as he studied the town ahead. His hat was uncomfortably tight. The long brown hair that straggled from beneath it was clean, but he felt unkempt. He'd been way too long away from town.

He'd stopped shaving more than a month ago. It wasn't the effort of it that bothered him. It wasn't the necessity of keeping his knife that sharp. It was always sharp enough to shave with. It was the necessary time spent staring into the small mirror that bothered him.

You can't shave with a large, very sharp knife without paying attention to your reflection. Unless you want to lose part of your nose, that is. You can't study your reflection and still watch the tree-line, the ridge tops, your horse's change of attitude — any of the things that would indicate someone approaching.

It was that ceaseless attention to tiny details that saved his life the morning he had decided not to shave. The Indian, a Crow on a trek of vengeance all the way from Montana, had managed to get to within less than a hundred feet of his camp unnoticed.

His dog didn't even detect the stealthy brave. Only his horse caught some movement, some scent, some faint glimmer of warning.

Even the horse made no sound. His head just came up abruptly. From the corner of his eye, Levi caught that unexpected movement. Without even thinking, he took a quick step backward as he rose from where he was squatted beside his fire. The Indian's rifle barked just as he moved. The bullet passed so close to his chest he could feel it and hear its angry hiss.

The Crow brave didn't get a second shot. With uncanny speed Levi's .45 leaped into his hand, spitting flame toward the source of the shot. One of the three closely spaced shots caught the Indian squarely as he levered a second shell into the rifle and sent him spinning backward. He was dead when he hit the ground.

The first thought that ran through Levi's mind was

6

that if he had been shaving, he probably wouldn't have noticed the horse's silent movement. He hadn't shaved since. At first the beard was scratchy and felt out of place. As he had gotten used to it, it stopped troubling him.

It bothered him now, though. He felt exactly what he must look like. His clothes were less than clean, and thoroughly worn. His beard and hair were unkempt. His saddle and his gear were in excellent repair, but even his hat was bedraggled and floppy. He could have passed for any of the countless drifters who went wherever the work was, on any ranch that was hiring. Their gear was always top notch, but their own person never received the same care. In a word, he looked like a range bum. A drifter.

Except for the guns.

Range bums didn't wear their guns like that. One was too low on the hip, tied down. A second gun, butt forward, rode his left side at belt-level. Just behind the left gun, a large knife fit snugly in its sheath.

Two scabbards graced the saddle instead of the one most cowhands had. The 30.30 rifle was in the one below his left leg, stock forward. On the other side of the saddle, stock toward the rear, a fatter scabbard held a twelve-gauge Colt revolving shotgun. Too many guns for a cowhand. The shotgun itself was a weapon no cowhand would ever carry. Its only purpose was the devastating firepower of a shotgun loaded with buckshot that could fire six times as rapidly as a six-shooter.

There was no hiding what he was. He was a gunman.

7

That cold fact, combined with his unkempt appearance, seemed to produce a visible wave in front of him, spreading out to either side. He often thought the effect would be exactly the same if he had tangled with a skunk, and come out the loser.

As he entered the town, those within that invisible vee-shaped wedge that preceded him stopped what they were doing or saying. They turned to watch him pass. He rode in that ripple of silence that seemed to follow wherever he went. When he was well past, he could hear conversations resume, often with an excited little murmur added.

Those with a past, or who might have something to fear from the law, or from bounty hunters, were instantly visible. Their eyes narrowed. Their steps slowed. Their hands dropped to brush the butt of their own gun. They always faced him squarely, turning as he rode past, to keep him straight in front of them until they decided he posed no personal threat.

As they walked away, they always cast at least one glance back over their shoulder.

He fought the bile that rose in his throat. They wanted him around badly enough when they were scared, when there was danger afoot. They appreciated his skill with those guns when they needed his protection. But they wanted him somewhere else as soon as the trouble was over. It was the same everywhere.

He wondered fleetingly what it would be like to walk down a street like this and know the sound of greetings and welcomes. He wondered how it would be never to wonder whether greetings called out were sincere. What would it be like to be someone people were comfortable with? He sighed and shrugged off the thought. That's one thing he would probably never know.

He reined in and tied up his horse in front of a two-story building boasting a sign that said: CHEER-FUL HOTEL.

He resisted the urge to sneer. 'With a cheerful desk-clerk and a cheerful bed, complete with a cheerful whore for an extra two dollars,' he muttered.

'Stay here, Curly,' he told the mottled yellow dog that watched him expectantly. Instantly the dog sat down beside the horse's front leg. The horse bent his head down to nuzzle the dog gently. Levi Hill strode into the hotel.

'Got a room facin' the street?'

'Dollar a day. Pay in advance.'

Levi tossed a ten-dollar gold piece on the desk.

'I'll pay ten days for now.'

'Plannin' on bein' here a while, huh?'

'Maybe. Where's the town marshal's office?'

'Block down. Same side o' the street. Got business with him, do you?'

Levi ignored the question, picked up the key and went upstairs. He checked out the room, returned to retrieve his things from his horse, and put them in the room. He stopped at the desk on the way out. He put on his best angry glare as he stared at the desk clerk.

'If anyone touches anything in that room, or even opens the door of it, I'll know, and I'll come lookin' for you.'

The desk clerk swallowed with obvious effort.

'We don't never have nothin' bothered in the rooms, mister.'

'See that it stays that way.'

He stepped into the saddle and turned away from the hitching-rail. The effect of his presence in the street resumed immediately, even though both saddle scabbards were now empty. For just an instant he had an almost irresistible urge to yell, 'Boo!' at those closest to him. Their reaction might be fun. He managed to restrain himself.

At the livery barn he paid a week's keep in advance and put his horse away.

'Stay with him, Curly,' he ordered the dog.

Obediently the dog curled up in a front corner of the horse's stall.

The walk to the marshal's office had the same effect as his ride down the street. For some reason, it niggled him more than normal. When he entered the marshal's office he was already struggling to control his anger.

'We ain't fond o' bounty hunters here in Cheerful,' the marshal announced before Levi was completely inside the door.

Levi stopped, his hand still on the doorknob. He fought down the response that rose instantly to his lips. Instead he said:

'Seen any o' them fellas lately?'

'What fellas?'

'Bounty hunters.'

'Lookin' at one now, if I'm any judge.'

'Well, we already know you ain't much of a judge, then.'

'Don't get smart.'

'I already did. I got smart a long time before I saw you. So far seein' you ain't made me any smarter. You the marshal?'

The marshal's face reddened. He moved his feet from the top of his desk and stood up. He was clearly six inches taller than the newcomer to his office. His mustache bristled.

'Yeah, I'm the marshal. An' you're jist about half a minute away from bein' a jailbird.'

'Really? You arrest people for not bowin' or kneelin' when they walk into your office these days?'

'I arrest people fer whatever I think they need arrestin' fer.'

'Well, maybe you'd best stop doin' that. I believe there's a small matter called "the law", that tells you who and when it's legal to arrest.'

'Oh, an expert on the law we have here, do we?'

Levi stepped clear of the door. His hand brushed the butt of the well-worn Colt .45 on his hip, then stayed there, barely touching it, but feeling its presence. His voice went flat and hard.

'Well, yeah, as a matter of fact we do. And I believe my badge outranks yours, for whatever that's worth. My name's Levi Hill. I'm a Pinkerton Detective. I'm also a Deputy United States Marshal. And yes, I am an expert on the law. Now would you like to stop bein' Mr Tough Guy and act civil, or would you rather I wrapped a gun barrel around your head and locked you in one of your own cells until you can learn to act civilized, when a man walks into your office?'

The marshal's expression changed as Levi spoke. The fiery anger in his face drained away, leaving an unnatural pallor behind. His eyes widened. His Adam's apple bobbed up and down. He sat back down. He cleared his throat nervously.

'Well, you don't have to go gettin' yer dander up. I had no way o' knowin' who ya was. What can I do fer ya?'

'You can start by being a little more civil. I'd have told you who I was if you hadn't called me a bounty hunter before I even got in the door.'

The marshal struggled to regain his bluster.

'Well, if'n you don't want to be called one, don't go 'round lookin' so dang much like one. A haircut an' a shave'd make ya look half-way respectable at least.'

Levi started to retort, then put a clamp on his tongue. The marshal didn't offer too long an opportunity for him to answer.

'What's Pinkerton buttin' its nose inta Cheerful fer?'

Levi took in a deep breath. In a voice much more hearty than the situation called for, he said:

'Why thank you, Marshal. Yes, I will have a chair. So nice of you to offer. Fine town you have here.'

He pulled a straight-back chair to the place he wanted it and sat down. He lifted a dusty boot and crossed it over his other knee. The marshal's scowl deepened.

'Didn't figger we had a chair good 'nuff fer Pinkerton's number one man-killer, but I guess ya kin make do. What ya want in Cheerful?'

12

Levi let silence hang for a long moment. In a deliberately conciliatory tone, he said:

'Tell you what. How about we start over, and see if we can get on each other's nerves a little less. I just have a job to do. I'm here to try to do it.'

'I got a job to do too. Keepin' Cheerful peace-able's a big part of it. I got a feelin' it ain't about to git any easier.'

'I'm not here to cause any trouble in town. Do you know Burton Shedd?'

The marshal grunted. ' 'Course I know Butch Shedd. You ain't lookin' fer him, are ya?'

'Only to talk to. He's the one that hired Pinkerton to look into a death.'

The marshal grunted again.

'He ain't gonna let it drop, huh? Went an' hired Pinkerton! Dang!'

'Is that a problem?'

'It ain't none o' my problem. Ain't no call him wastin' good money thataway, though. Pinkerton! You think you kin figger out anythin' more'n what I figgered out, yer welcome. I 'spect it's 'bout the kid?'

'The one that worked for him. Lester Farmington. What can you tell me about it?'

'Danged little. Found 'im lyin' behind his house. 'Twixt the house an' the shed. Head was split wide open with a double-bitted axe. Axe was still right there, still stuck in 'is head. His own axe, even. Looked like whoever done it come up behind him. Don't figger he ever seen it comin'. Fer dang sure he never felt nothin'. Split clean through his head. Blade o' the axe was stuck plumb inta his neck-bone, all the way down through his head. Somebody give it a right good swing. O' course, we ain't nigh as smart as Pinkerton 'round here, but we figgered as how he was sure dead all right, an' by detective work thet was pertneart genius we reasoned out that most likely somebody done kilt 'im.'

Levi ignored the barbs. 'Did he have any enemies that you know about?'

'One, anyway.'

'Who?'

'Whoever it was what split his head open.'

'That's helpful.'

'Ain't tryin' ta be helpful, in case ya ain't noticed. Don't s'pose ya care none 'bout Walters.'

'Who's Walters?'

'Luther Walters.'

'Who's Luther Walters?' Levi obliged, fighting to keep his temper in check.

'Who *was* Luther Walters?' the marshal corrected. 'He ain't no more. He was a fella with a small ranch up north o' here a ways. Somebody shot 'im offa his horse. Pertneart cut 'im in two with a load o' buckshot. Both barrels, looked like.'

Levi waited for more information, but none came forth.

'Any idea who shot him?'

'Nope.'

Levi waited a long moment, chaffing at the lawman's attitude. Eventually he rose from his chair.

'Well, if you get to bubblin' over with information and enthusiasm and can't contain yourself, I'll be around.'

14

'Now thet's a pity.'

Pity was not the emotion that roiled within Levi as he strode out.

CHAPTER 2

Levi stood outside the marshal's office, forcing his emotions back into check. The immediate effect his appearance had on the townspeople didn't help. Some stared with open curiosity. Others scowled their disapproval of his presence. He sighed and pulled his too-tight hat down. He began to walk along the board sidewalk.

'You're not from around here.'

He stopped and turned around at the voice. A middle-aged woman with a shape like a too-full sack of potatoes stood on the board sidewalk, hands on her hips, frankly appraising him.

'That's a fact, ma'am,' Levi responded, touching the front of his hat.

'You're a gunman.' It was a statement rather than a question.

'In a manner of speaking, that's true enough,' he agreed.

'Why would a gunman be interested in Cheerful?'

'Why does my presence trouble you?' he countered.

'Because we have a nice, peaceful town here. We don't need trouble. Your kind always bring nothing but trouble. We have trouble enough of our own already.'

Levi frowned, seeming to struggle with her words.

'Now, pardon me, ma'am, but I don't understand that. You say this is a nice, peaceful town that already has too much trouble. If it's nice and peaceful, how can it have that much trouble? On the other hand, if it has that much trouble, how can it be nice and peaceful? Whenever there's some sort of a fight here, do folks say: "Excuse me", every time they hit each other?'

The woman turned beet-red and glared back at him.

'You aren't welcome in Cheerful,' she insisted.

'Really? And who decided that? Are you the official Cheerful not-welcome committee? If you are, you really must learn to do more on the Cheerful part of it. You know, smile sweetly when you tell folks they're not welcome. You could give Cheerful a bad name, otherwise.'

Emitting a loud 'harump', she wheeled and walked away.

'Well, by Jing, that's the first time I ever seen anyone get the last word on Ma Ferguson.'

Levi turned at the words. A grizzled oldster leaned against a store front. Levi smiled tightly.

'Shame she's so bashful about saying what she means,' he observed. The oldster chuckled again.

'She's a caution all right. You be lookin' fer someone in partickler?'

17

Levi eyed the man carefully. He was as lean as a whip and, if Levi were any judge, every bit as tough. He was rolling a cigarette paper around tobacco that had been carefully arranged along its length. His hands were steady. The well-worn pistol on his hip was clearly there for more than decoration. He instantly liked the man. He grinned.

'Well, right now I think what I need to be lookin' for first is a good barber, then I need to find Burton Shedd.'

The old man eyed him with exaggerated appraisal.

'Yeah, you could use a good barber. Too bad we ain't got one. We got a fair-ta-middlin' one, though. Keep on goin' down this sidewalk, ya'll find 'im 'bout six doors down.'

'Thanks. How about Shedd?'

'You be friend er foe?'

'Friend. He's the one that sent for me.'

'Now why would Butch send fer a gunman?'

'I'm a lawman. Pinkerton.'

'Aaaah! Now thet thar makes a heap more sense. Lookin' inta the murder o' thet clerk o' his, I reckon.'

'I reckon.'

'Well, in that case, he's the one thet owns the mercantile store. Down the street over there on t'other side. Cain't miss it.'

'Thanks.'

'Glad yer a lawman.'

'Why's that?'

'Well, we could use a good lawman fer a while, fer one thing. Fer t'other, I'd like to think good of a man what got the last word on Ma Ferguson. Kinda hard to think good of a gunfighter. If 'n he ain't a lawman, I mean.'

'You look like you might be a bit handy with a gun yourself.'

The old man's eyes twinkled. 'Thet's what I mean. I ain't no lawman.'

'My name's Levi Hill,' Levi said, extending a hand.

The oldster took it in an iron grip. 'Is that so? Well, thet explains some. Heard about ya. I'm Capt'n Renfro.'

'Jesse Renfro?'

'The same.'

'I've heard of you, too. Glad to make your acquaintance. I didn't know you were still in the country.'

'Well, prob'ly jist as well ya don't go blabbin' it all over Wyoming. Most folks figger I went back to Texas an' dried up lonesome, sittin' next to a cactus like ol' Rangers is supposed to do. Truth is, I bought me a little spread over east a little ways. Got me a nice little herd an' a good woman. Sorta blendin' inta the scenery, ya know?'

Levi nodded. 'It must be workin'. I ain't heard your name mentioned for several years.'

'Ya git over east 'bout eleven miles, my place is at the head of a big wide, shallow draw jist under the flat-topped mountain. Drop in an' visit.'

'I'll do that. Thanks.'

He strode down the street and stepped into the barber-shop.

'Well now, there's a good customer,' the barber said, getting up from his own barber-chair. 'I like to see a man that really needs a good haircut. Shame to waste a good one on a man that don't really need it.'

'You charge him the same, though, I bet. I figured to get my money's worth. Shave too. Leave the mustache, but trim it up so it looks civilized.'

'Like to keep that scar on your lip covered, huh?'

Levi looked at the barber appreciatively.

'You've got a keen eye. Under that much brush, I wouldn't think you'd notice.'

'Well, if you was missin' an arm, I might not. Hair'n beards are my business, though. Man tends to notice things he deals with. How'd you get your lip messed up that bad?'

'Fella took a shot at me once. Pertneart didn't miss.'

'Too close for me, I can tell you that. Mustache covers it up good, though. Doesn't seem to affect your talkin'.'

'Good thing. I'd hate to have to be at that much of a disadvantage when I'm tryin' to keep up with a barber.'

As he slid into the chair the barber, chuckling at the comment, spread an apron over him, pinning it behind his neck.

'Keep the chair pointed toward the street, would you?' Levi requested. 'I kinda like to see who's comin'.'

'I can do that,' the barber agreed. His voice was affable to the point of being artificially jovial. 'I hate having a customer get shot while he's in the chair. It makes such a mess to clean up. Then I can't take care of any more customers till they get him drug out and everything. Messes up a day something awful. Besides, that means I'm not apt to get paid for that one. I hate it when that happens after I've done all the work, and I still don't get paid.'

'Yeah, well, I wouldn't want to be guilty of that, so I'll keep my eyes peeled. Makin' sure you get your money is the only reason I really care, you understand.'

'Downright considerate of you. I like a man that's considerate of my business. Passing through, or going to be in town a while?'

Over the next half-hour the barber kept up a light-hearted patter, while he took several months' worth of head and facial hair from Levi. His face felt naked and vulnerable as he stood up and put his hat back on. The hat dropped clear to his ears.

The barber pulled out a long strip of the paper from the roll he used to wrap around his customer's neck beneath the apron.

'Here. Fold this lengthwise and put this under your hatband to tighten up your hat till your hair grows back out some.'

'You sure do take the size of a man's head down a notch, don't you?'

'Yeah, sometimes. Now it's gonna take me the rest of the day to get all this extra hair swept up off the floor and haul it out. Shame a man can't make something out of it.'

'They make saddle blankets out of horse-hair.'

'So they do. I wonder if it'd work to use human hair?'

'I'll leave that to you to figure out. But if you make

'em and sell 'em, I get half for the idea.' Levi grinned as he paid the man and left.

A small bell attached to the front door jingled as Levi stepped into the mercantile store. A cheerful, female voice called out from the back:

'I'll be right with you.'

'No hurry,' Levi called back.

He busied himself looking over the store's surprising profusion of merchandise as he waited. He was looking at pants made of heavy denim material that was almost like canvas, as the clerk came to wait on him.

'Need a pair of the new Levi Strauss pants? They wear forever.'

He turned to look at the speaker and caught his breath. She wasn't really what he would have described as pretty. She was striking. She was almost exactly his own height. Her hair was dark brown. Her eyes were large and dark, sparkling with intelligence, humor, and an almost brazen forwardness as she met his gaze evenly. She neither blinked, nor batted her eyelashes. Still, there was no challenge there. Only a very frank matching of his own gaze. Her long dark hair cascaded across unusually broad shoulders. There was no fat on her full figure, but all the right places were filled out to perfection. That open frankness in her face, unusual as it was in women, was almost intimidating. She looked him up and down with no apparent self-consciousness at all. He was suddenly glad he had stopped for a haircut and shave before he got to the store.

'I've had a couple pair of them,' he said. 'They're

good. Do you cut and hem the legs?'

She smiled at him. For reasons he couldn't fathom, it seemed like the world brightened immensely when she did.

'Sure do. That's about the only way you'd find any with short enough legs, isn't it?'

He grinned. 'Noticed that already, huh? You see, I was supposed to be seven feet tall, but my ma got tired before she got the legs finished.'

Her smile broadened. 'I'm glad she quit when she did. I hate to get a crick in my neck looking up at someone I want to look at. Would you like a pair of these?'

'Yes, I would. Do you need me to try them on to get the length?'

'I don't think so. I'm pretty good at guessing them right. I can have them ready by tomorrow.'

'That'll be fine. Is Burton Shedd in?'

'Butch? Sure. Shall I tell him who wants to see him?'

'Yeah, if you know.'

She smiled again. Her eyes danced.

'Oh, I'll know all right, just as soon as you tell me.'

Any offense his words might have spawned was offset by the matching twinkle in his own eyes.

'Does he always have you quiz folks that want to see him?'

'No. He never does, as a matter of fact. I asked because I want to know, and that seemed easier than saying: "Who are you?" '

His grin opened to match hers that time. 'Fair enough. My name's Levi Hill. I work for Pinkerton.

23

Now it's your turn.'

'Oh! You're the detective he's been waiting for. He'll be glad you're here. I'll get him.'

'Well now wait a minute! You didn't answer my question yet.'

'I didn't hear you ask one.'

'I, well, I didn't. But I did say it was your turn. But I can put it as a question. To whom do I have the distinct pleasure of directing this unusually enjoyable repartee?'

'Well! With flawless grammar, no less! My name is Myra Funderburke.'

'And is that Mrs or Miss Funderburke?'

'It's Myra.'

After she let that hang in a long moment of silence, she continued: 'But there isn't a Mr Funderburke, other than my father, if that's what you're asking.'

'Well, then, after I've talked with Mr Shedd, may I have the pleasure of your company for supper at the doubtless Cheerful purveyor of fine foods?'

'I'm sorry. I never see the store's customers socially.'

'Cancel the order for those pants. Now I'm not a customer, so will you have supper with me?'

She laughed merrily. 'How could I refuse after all that? We close the store at seven. And you don't really need to cancel the order for the pants.'

'Good. A couple more weeks' worth of wear, and these I've got on are going to get embarrassing.'

'I doubt it. I don't embarrass that easily. I'll get Mr Shedd.'

He watched her walk away. She walked with a long stride, with no affectation, no artificial swing of her hips. He had never met a woman so totally without any of the small pretenses that women used to try to make themselves attractive, or coy, or to seem shy. She was so open and frank, without coquettishness or feminine wiles, yet so totally and stunningly feminine, that it nearly took his breath away.

A small man hurried down the aisle of the store toward him. He had a pair of spectacles perched on his nose, and walked with his head tipped down so he could see over them.

'Levi Hill?' he asked, extending his hand.

'You'd be Mr Shedd?'

'Butch,' he corrected him. 'Just Butch. I'm glad you're here. Are you staying at the hotel, or will you be staying with my wife and me?'

'I've got a room at the hotel.'

'Very well. May I invite you to supper? We can discuss the particulars of why I have engaged Pinkerton's agency over a good meal.'

'Well, I, uh, sorta have an engagement for supper tonight.'

His eyebrows shot up. He glanced over where Myra was straightening things on a shelf, then back again. 'Am I to understand that my clerk agreed to have supper with you? On your first day in town?'

'Well, yeah. She did, as a matter of fact.'

'Why, I declare! I've heard her turn down fifty invitations at least, and she accepted yours. My, my! Well, if you will forgive me, I will simply invite Myra to accompany you, and your supper with her won't cost

CHAPTER 3

'I have to apologize again for that puncher's obnoxious behavior.'

Levi shrugged, smiling at Myra. 'No need for you to apologize. It wasn't you that called me a hired killer. You didn't even ask me to leave town. For which I'm glad, by the way.'

Myra chuckled. 'I've never heard anyone called that so nicely before.'

'Called what?' Butch asked.

Myra glanced at Mrs Shedd, obviously making a decision whether to share the whole conversation at the supper table. Her decision was just as evident. She laid her fork down and leaned forward. She directed her explanation to the Shedds. Her eyes danced.

'When Levi was in the store, after he'd talked with you, Bucky Denton came in. He's such a self-righteous prig he makes me sick anyway! He looked at Levi, and said: 'When you buy what you need, why don't you leave Cheerful? We don't need hired killers around here.'

'He said that?' Wilhelmina gasped. 'Without even knowing him?'

'He said that,' Myra assured her. 'And Levi looked at him almost like he was a spider on his plate, and in the nicest, sweetest, quiet voice, said: "Tell me, sir: if the rest of the horse turned around and went the other direction, would you become something different, or would you simply become the south end when he went north?" '

Wilhelmina snorted, sending coffee up her nose, making her turn abruptly away from the table. She gasped back into a semblance of control. Her eyebrows remained where they had shot up. Her mouth sagged open. After a few seconds she erupted in a gale of laughter. She laughed so hard tears welled in her eyes. She dabbed at them with her napkin.

'I've never,' she gasped as she tried to control her mirth, 'never heard anyone called a horse's, ah, behind, that cleverly. Whatever did he say?'

'It took him almost half a minute to figure out what he'd been called,' Myra chortled. 'He stood there with his mouth open for the whole time. Then he shut his mouth. He turned as red as a beet. I thought for a minute he was going to take a swing at Levi, and I was really hoping he would. I'd love to see him get the pompous stuffing beat out of him. But he didn't. He just turned around and stomped out of the store.'

Butch affected an artificial glare at Levi, belied by the twinkle in his eyes.

'In the future, Mr Hill, I would appreciate it if you

would insult my customers after they have made their purchases. I do have a business to maintain.'

Levi smiled. 'I'll try to control myself. I hate to change the subject, but how about we get down to why you hired Pinkerton.'

The mood at the table changed instantly, dropping from merriment to an almost somber heaviness in the space of a heartbeat.

'How much do you already know?'

'Not a whole lot. I stopped in and talked with your local marshal. Not what I'd call a friendly fella.'

It was Myra who responded first. The words shot out of her mouth as if propelled by pent-up steam.

'He's the poorest excuse of a lawman any town was ever cursed with. He is exactly what he's named. A crumb.'

Butch swiftly interrupted the tirade. 'Eugene Krumm is not in the finest tradition of lawmen, I'll admit. He does keep a pretty fair lid on Cheerful. He doesn't like any outside interference, though. He even gets in a huff if Harm stops in to check on things.'

'Who's Harm?'

'Harm Danver. He's the County Sheriff. Good man. Swings by from time to time, just to keep tabs on things. Gene always thinks he's being judged when he does, though. He usually invites Harm to leave town.'

'Nice to know I'm not the only one. There's a decided prejudice in this town, I've noticed though, against anyone who wears a gun.'

'At least against the ones who look like they know

how to use one,' Butch agreed.

'Sorta belies the town's name.'

'It does for a fact. There is not much cheer in Cheerful, most o' the time, I'm afraid.'

'Anyway, back to why you hired Pinkerton.'

'Ah, yes. I guess we have to deal with that, don't we? I had a clerk for several years, whose name was Lester Farmington. Fine young man. Really fine! Me an' 'Meena took to him right off. He wasn't more than seventeen or eighteen when he drifted into town. Orphan boy. Wanted a job. Wasn't put together to be a cowhand. Slight-built, you know. I hired him, and for a long time he lived here with us as well. He took to the business like nobody I ever saw. Natural at it. Honest as the day is long. He liked people, and the customers all liked him. He came to be just like a son to us. As a matter of fact, that's how we started thinking of him. He just became that son we never could have.'

A tear slid down Wilhelmina's cheek. She dabbed at it silently with a napkin. Butch fell silent, lost in a reverie whose pain was reflected in his eyes.

After a long silence Levi said: 'I'm sorry. What happened?'

Butch took a long, ragged breath. He tore himself from the memory he had lost himself in. He lifted a hand, then let it drop. The act resonated with helplessness.

'Somebody killed him. That's all I can tell you.'

After waiting for more information that was not forthcoming, Levi asked:

'At the store?'

Butch shook his head. 'No. He'd rented a small house about a block from the store. He had decided it was time he was more on his own than he felt living here. He'd lived there just over a year. Oh, he ate with us, most evenings. He was still just like a son. He just wanted to be a bit independent, you know. Young men are like that, I guess.'

After another silence, Levi probed: 'Is that where he was killed?'

Butch started as if wakened from a light nap. 'What? Oh. Oh, yes. Well, behind the house. It appeared that he had been riding somewhere. His horse had been rubbed down, but the saddle blanket was still sweaty. There's a shed behind the house where he kept his horse and things. He was almost to the back door of the house. Somebody came up behind him and used the axe from his own woodpile to kill him. He hadn't been dead too long when we found him. When he didn't come for supper, I went over to see if he was all right. I found him.'

Levi waited a respectful moment before he pursued it further. Wilhelmina turned from the table and blew her nose as delicately as possible.

'Any idea who might have done it?'

Butch shook his head. The hand lifted and dropped into his lap again.

'Not one lonesome idea in this whole wide world. I've thought about it almost non-stop from that day to this. I absolutely can't think of anyone who ever had a cross word with him, or said anything bad about him, or that didn't like him. He was just as fine a young man as you'll ever find. That's what makes it so hard. It just doesn't make any sense at all. He absolutely didn't have an enemy in the world.'

Levi resisted the urge to say: *Well, he obviously had one.* Instead he said:

'Do you have any idea where he'd been riding?'

Butch shook his head. 'No.'

'What day of the week was it?'

'Sunday.'

'So the store was closed?'

'Well, yes. That's why he was out riding. He went riding up in the mountains pretty nearly every Sunday.'

'Was he sweet on anyone? Any chance he was off seeing a woman somewhere?'

Butch shook his head again. 'Not that we know of. He talked to us about almost everything, and he didn't ever mention having a hankering for anyone. And no woman showed up at the funeral looking grieved. We were watching to see. If he was sweet on anyone, she'd surely have come to his funeral.'

'Unless she was married,' Levi suggested softly.

Both Butch and Wilhelmina started. They stared at him with widened eyes. Wilhelmina shook her head vigorously.

'Oh my, no! Not Les! No! No, he wouldn't ever have even looked at a married woman, let alone done anything more than look. He just wasn't that kind, at all. He really was a good boy, through and through.'

Levi and Myra exchanged a glance, and Levi dropped the matter. They left the table. He and Butch retired to the sitting-room while Myra and

32

Wilhelmina cleared the table and did the dishes. When they finished, they joined the men in the sitting-room, and visited for another hour.

Levi was delighted in the way Myra felt free to enter into the conversation, expressing her opinions with no hesitation. It was a distinct pleasure to talk about any subject that came up, with her included in the conversation.

'Well, I 'spect I'd best get back to the hotel,' Levi said at last.

At once Myra said: 'Would you mind walking me home on your way?'

'I'd be delighted,' he answered, hoping his voice didn't betray his enthusiasm too badly.

They walked slowly, engrossed in conversation the whole way. He shared with her that his sister was also named Myra. She shared her feelings about living in the house Lester Farmington had lived in until he was killed.

He didn't realize until he had said good night to her and was back at the hotel that he didn't have any idea where she had come from, how she came to be working for the Shedds, or anything at all about her background.

Oh well. That left plenty to talk about the next chance he got.

CHAPTER 4

The small dust cloud showed starkly against the deep blue of the sky.

'Somebody's in a big hurry,' Levi observed.

He stopped reluctantly. He was almost to the mercantile store, and the thought of having an excuse to talk with Myra quickened his pulse. He really didn't want a distraction. At the same time, a horse approaching town on a dead run couldn't be ignored.

His approach had obviously been noted from the store.

'What are you watching?' Myra called to him from the door.

Levi looked around and felt his heart skip a beat at the sight of Myra, half-way out the door of the store. He nodded in the general direction of the road.

'Somebody comin' in a big hurry.

'Then it won't be good news,' Myra observed. 'Nobody runs their horse in this heat with good news.'

She stepped out on to the sidewalk and stood beside him. She shielded her eyes from the sun with her hand. As they watched, a horse and rider appeared at the top of a rise a quarter of a mile from town. He was bent low over the saddle. His hatbrim was blown up by the wind of his horse's speed, plastered against the front of the hat's crown. He was straining forward as if to make the horse go faster by the force of his will.

After a minute Myra said: 'Spider Schultz.'

'Know him?'

'Not real well. He works for the Box-3.'

The cowboy passed them in a cloud of dust, hauling his horse to a stop in front of the marshal's office. He leaped from the horse and sprinted to the door. It was locked. He began to beat on it furiously.

Levi walked quickly to the marshal's office, arriving just as Krumm opened the door.

'Don't knock the door down!' Krumm remonstrated with the agitated cowboy. 'I'm gettin' here as fast as I kin.'

'Marshal! You gotta come! Will's been kilt!'

Krumm scowled. 'Will who?'

'Will Steiger. He rides with me on the Box-3. He's been kilt.'

'Whatd'ya mean, he's been kilt?'

'I mean he's been kilt! Somebody kilt 'im.'

'Shot 'im?'

'No. No, I don't think so. Looked like he beat 'im with somethin'. His head's all mashed up somethin' awful. You gotta come, Marshal!'

'Where is he?'

'Four, five miles out, along the crick.'

'I'm a town marshal, not a county sheriff. That's outa my jurisdiction.'

'But it's too far ta be ridin' clear over ta Laramie ta git the sheriff! Ya gotta come, Marshal!'

'All right. All right. I'll get a buckboard ta haul 'im inta town on, an' be along.'

Levi spoke up. 'Mind if I ride out with him and look it over while you're doin' that?'

The marshal glared at Levi as if he had been unaware of his presence.

'Now why would the almighty Pinkerton man wanta poke 'is nose inta this?'

Levi shrugged, trying to act nonchalant.

'Might be a connection. Three murders in a place as nice and friendly as Cheerful in that length of time prob'ly ain't a coincidence.'

Krumm shrugged in response. 'It's a free country. Ride where ya want. 'Sides, ya already made sure I know your badge is bigger'n mine. I reckon ya got more jurisdiction out there'n I do. Ain't much sense in me messin' with it atall, what with a famous expert like you bein' involved.'

Levi ignored the animosity and bitterness.

'We won't move anything till you get there with the buckboard,' he said. He turned to the cowboy and, ignoring the marshal, added: 'You'll be wantin' a fresh horse too, I 'spect. You can get one at the livery barn while I get saddled up.'

'Yeah. Yeah, thet'll be good. Yeah. I kin borry one o' Gimpy's an' leave mine there. I did ride 'im plumb hard.'

Levi and Spider rode out at a brisk trot some fifteen minutes later.

The murder scene was a picture of irenic beauty, except for the glaringly incongruous body crumpled in an awkward heap in the middle of it. Tall cotton-woods framed a quiet glen beside a trickle of a stream. Through the branches of the large-leafed trees, tall mountains formed a backdrop. A saddled horse stood with reins dragging, cropping grass and swishing its tail at the pesky flies. A squirrel chattered from a tree-branch.

In the center of the clearing a small fire had been built. A branding-iron still lay in it, though the wood had long since burned away and the ashes had grown cold. A short piece of rope lay nearby.

At the edge of the clearing, Levi held up a hand.

'Don't ride any closer till I have a look around,' he requested.

Spider nodded. He leaned forward in the saddle, both hands on the saddle horn. He hadn't spoken since they had left Cheerful, and didn't do so now. He looked as if he'd burst out crying if he tried to talk.

Levi dismounted and began a slow, careful circle of the clearing. Three times he stopped, studied the ground, then moved out of sight back into the trees, watching the ground closely. The last time he did so, he emerged, again on a different side of the clearing, still studying the ground minutely.

Still watching the ground, he approached the body. He looked at it and the ground around it for a long time. Eventually he called out to the cowboy.

'All right, Spider. You can come on over now.'

Spider rode forward slowly. 'How'd you know my name?'

'Myra told me.'

'Who?'

'Myra. The woman who works for Shedd.'

'Oh. Yeah. Yeah, I 'spect she'd know me, all right. Buy my stuff in there. She took Les's place. What'd ya find? You a tracker?'

'Yeah. Will was your friend?'

'Yup. Yup, he sure was. Best friend I ever had. Rode with 'im three years fer the Bar-70. Spent a year prospectin' together. Didn't never find much. Been ridin' together fer the Box-3 better'n two years. Now somebody went an' kilt 'im, and I don't even know how come.'

'He have any enemies that you know of?'

'Naw. He didn't mess with nobody. Some fellas is always pullin' stunts on the other hands, you know, stuff like thet. Not Will. He never did.'

'Have a woman?'

'What d'ya mean? Like married er somethin'?'

'He wasn't married, was he?'

'Naw.'

'Have a lady-friend?'

'Naw. Oh, he kidded most anyone a little. Women, I mean. Jist good-natured kiddin', ya know. 'Bout bein' nice-lookin'. Stuff like thet. But if he actchly needed a woman, we'd jist go inta town. They's always a whore at the Dusty Soul. Two er three, usually. Naw, he warn't sweet on no one.'

'Well, somebody sure had it in for him.'

38

'Why d'ya say thet?'

'Well, somebody followed him here. I'll ride back along his trail while you wait for the marshal, then I'll know how far he followed him. But he was followin' 'im when he rode up here. Will spotted a calf, it looks like, that wasn't branded. Roped 'im. Tied 'im up. Made a fire to heat his brandin'-iron. Whoever was followin' 'im waited over there in the trees, watchin'. I 'spect the calf's mama was worryin' Will some. She did a lot o' pacin' back an' forth, over there. While he was watchin' her, and watchin' his brandin'-iron, whoever followed him walked up behind him and hit him with a big hunk of tree-limb. That hunk lyin' over there. Whoever it was sure didn't like 'im. Plumb mad.'

'Why d'ya say thet?'

'He must've hit him a dozen times with that club. The first one had to've knocked 'im out. Maybe killed him outright. Skull's dented in quite a ways. But he kept poundin' on 'im till he mashed his head to pieces. Then he must've turned the calf loose. Maybe it wasn't a Box-3 calf.'

'It was.'

'It was? How do you know?'

'I turned it loose. It was still tied up when I found 'im. The cow was still messin' with it, tryin' to get it to get up an' come along. I didn't wanta leave it hogtied while I went to town. I knowed I couldn't do nothin' fer Will. I could see he was plumb deader'n a doornail. His horse wasn't goin' nowheres, but he could eat all right, even with the bridle on. So I turned the calf loose and rode fer town.'

'Well, it wasn't because he was runnin' a long rope, then. Somebody was sure mad at 'im. Well, I'll backtrack 'im and the guy that killed him. I'll see if I can find out where he started followin' 'im. That might tell me why. The marshal'll take the body to town. You wanta wait with Will, or ride with me?'

'Oh, I guess I'll sorta stay here. I already left Will alone once. He hadn't oughta have ta wait here all by hisself. I mean, I guess it don't matter none ta him no more, but it sorta does ta me, ya know?'

'Sure. One other thing. Would you mind checking his pockets and his horse for me?'

'Fer what?'

'To see if anything's been stolen.'

'Ya think it mighta been jist ta rob 'im?'

'I don't know. I doubt it, but it's a possibility. He's still wearing his gun, and if someone wanted to rob him, they'd most likely have taken it. But check anyway, would you?'

Spider stepped from his horse. His too-long, gangly legs seemed almost to fold and unfold, propelling his body across the clearing. He crouched beside his friend.

'Sorry, Will. Ain't tryin' ta snoop. Gotta check, though, ya know.'

He emptied the cowhand's pockets. They contained three gold coins, a large pocket-knife, two rattlesnake rattles, and a hard, dry biscuit.

'His money's here,' Spider announced.

He unfolded from the ground and stretched himself over to where Will's horse continued to try to munch grass around the bit in his mouth. He checked the saddle-bags quickly. 'Ain't nothin' been bothered atall, near's I kin tell.'

Levi nodded. 'All right. That's what I figured. Thanks. You'll be at the Box-3 if I need to look you up to ask any more questions?'

Spider pushed his hat up from the back of his head and scratched his head thoughtfully.

'Wal, I hadn't much thought 'bout thet. I 'spect . . . Wal, I dunno. Naw, I sorta doubt it. I ain't sure I could much tolerate bein' there without Will around. I ain't like ta miss 'im as much, if'n I ain't where I'm used to him bein', ya know? I'm most likely ta draw my time an' drift somewheres. I got seven, eight months' pay comin'. Maybe I'll sorta hang around Cheerful fer a spell.'

Levi nodded and stepped wordlessly into the saddle. He headed out at a trot, watching the trail few men could have seen, let alone followed at a trot.

He was sure it was a wild-goose chase. He would find where the one hunting Will had spotted him, see the tracks as he followed, waiting for the opportunity. But somewhere before he began to follow, and somewhere after the deed was done, his trail would meld into some well-traveled road and be lost.

At least it beat hanging around Cheerful. He had never been in a town so eager to condemn him for a gunman and a killer. On the other hand, there was Myra. Now there was a woman! But even her presence couldn't keep his mood from being soured by the constant barrage of insults and snubs.

'Most misnamed town I ever heard of,' he groused.

CHAPTER 5

Unwashed body odor didn't help.

Levi turned slightly away from the new arrival at the Dusty Soul saloon. He looked around the room again, hoping a table had emptied. He hated standing at the bar.

Aside from the awkward perch, standing at the bar required him to watch the patrons of the saloon in the mirror behind the bar. It left far too many blind spots. He was only at ease when he had his back to the wall, with the whole of the saloon in his range of vision.

Standing at the bar also made it harder to nurse a single beer for a couple hours, without it being overly obvious. He toyed briefly with the idea of abandoning that long-standing rule. He could stand to tie one on.

Too many years of conditioning wouldn't allow it, however. He could not allow his reflexes to be compromised. He knew too many men who had died because the booze had simply made their hand a split second too slow, their aim a few inches errant.

The big man crowded against him, shoving him sideways. Levi scowled, trying to ignore the rising tide of irritation within him.

On a better day, or a better week, he could have done so. The events of the past week had taken a toll, however. The constant insults and snubs of the town had really gotten under his hide. The picture in his mind of a cowboy, bludgeoned from behind, his head battered into a pile of bloody mush, wouldn't leave his mind. He was hot, angry, frustrated, and in no mood to be crowded by an oversized range bum that smelled like he had rolled with the dogs in some decaying carcass.

'You gonna drink that beer er just hold it?'

He looked up at the bartender. His voice was sharper than he intended.

'Does it matter to you?'

The bartender didn't flinch. His voice was friendly and reasonable, but firm.

'Purty crowded. You're takin' up room at the bar.'

Levi bit his tongue. He knew the man was right. He wasn't willing to let that dictate his own behavior.

'How 'bout you dump this one an' bring me a fresh one.'

'Fair enough,' the bartender agreed.

He took the beer and tossed it into a bucket, refilled the mug and set it back in front of Levi. He took the money and moved on down the bar.

'Your momma lets ya hold it, but won't let ya drink it, is that it?'

Levi's blood pressure rose another notch. He glanced up briefly at the leering face beside him. He decided to ignore it. His gaze scanned the crowded room by means of the mirror. A sharp elbow in the ribs snatched his attention back.

'I asked ya a question,' the big man insisted. Levi gave him a withering look.

'I heard the question. I thought it was too dumb to bother with.'

Small gasps escaped the lips of three or four nearby patrons of the saloon. They began to inch away from Levi and the man beside him.

'What'd you say?'

'Maybe you oughta try cleanin' a pound or two o' dirt outa your ears, 'less you're plannin' on growin' spuds in 'em. Then you could hear me.'

The attention of those closest was riveted on the two. At the last statement, the circle of those listening and watching grew. The noise in the saloon began to fade to an expectant hush.

'You callin' me dirty?'

'My nose made that announcement when you walked in the front door. I 'spect everybody else's has too, by now.'

An instant of deathly silence betrayed the man's incredulity that anyone would talk to him that way. It took only a second or two.

'You wanta step outside an' say that, little man?'

'Nope.'

Levi stepped back half a step. His hand still rested on the top of the bar. The big man turned to face him, still at something of a loss to figure out what was happening. He never really knew.

A week of intense frustration suddenly had a

convenient vent. All of it poured into the fist that formed in mid-swing. The overhand right that came from his shoulder picked up the force of the powerful shoulder behind it, augmented by the deceptive strength in the too-short legs that anchored him to the floor. By the time it reached the big man's chin, it had all the force of his amazing strength, coupled with a temper too long held in check.

The fist connected with the unsuspecting chin with the sound of a sledge hammer on a fence post. The shock of it traveled back down Levi's arm. He felt it clear to the ball of his right foot which had propelled him forward.

The big man didn't move. For just an instant, Levi thought he was impervious to the blow. Then he saw his eyes slowly lose focus and cross.

Acting much more nonchalant than he felt, he turned back to the bar and took hold of his mug of beer. As he did, the man began to totter. He leaned slowly backward, picking up speed as he went. Everyone behind him was clear of his trajectory as he toppled. He went down with a thud. Sawdust splayed out from beneath him as he landed, one arm draped limply across the brass rail at the base of the bar.

The deathly silence reined for several more seconds, then gave way to an excited babble of sound.

'Did you see that?'

'I never seen Ike down afore.'

'He ain't movin', neither.'

'He didn't even watch to see 'im fall. He jist went back to 'is beer.'

46

'I ain't never seen anyone hit that hard in my life.'

'I wouldn't wanta be that fella when Ike comes to.'

'Ya think he'll come to?'

'Why not? You reckon he's dead?'

'He ain't movin'.'

'Who's the little guy?'

'He ain't little. He's jist short.'

'He ain't all that short. He jist looks it alongside Ike.'

'Everyone looks short alongside Ike.'

'He's right, though. Ike's been needin' a bath some.'

'That's puttin' it mildly.'

' 'Spect he'll git one now?'

'Who is that guy?'

'Been nosin' around the past week.'

'That so? What about?'

'Ain't sure. Asks a lot o' questions, I hear.'

'Yeah? What kinda questions?'

'Ain't sure. Jist heard he asks a lot o' questions. Gunman, looks like.'

'Gunfighters don't fight with their fists. Makes their hands stiff.'

'Well, he sure does. Not much of a fight though. Knocked Ike out with one punch!'

Only half-hearing the hubbub of voices, Levi watched the big man out of the corner of his eye. After a few minutes, he began to stir. At last he sat up. He looked around, blinking rapidly. He shook his head, then obviously regretted it immediately.

'What happened?' he muttered.

'You got busted,' a voice advised him.

'Huh?'

'You got hit.'

'I got hit? Who by?'

'Me,' Levi said.

The big man blinked up at him. His mind began to function, as memory returned.

'Ya cold-cocked me?'

'Either that or you decided to lie down an' take a nap.'

'Why, you smart-mouthed . . .'

He rolled over and lumbered to his feet, then stood swaying as the room obviously spun around him. Levi watched, smiling tightly.

'You best go somewhere, take a bath, sleep a while, then come back if you wanta push it,' he advised.

The big man shook his head to clear it. It didn't. It made the dizziness worse. Muttering to himself, he stumbled out the door.

Levi waited until the patrons of the saloon returned to their own concerns. He toyed with the idea of going back to the hotel, but the idea didn't come to fruition.

Marshal Krumm stepped in the door of the saloon. A Greener double-barreled shotgun hung loosely in his right hand.

'What's goin' on in here?'

An excited hubbub of voices all tried to tell him at once. He held up a hand.

'All right, all right! I can't hear everybody at once. Fred, tell me what's goin' on.'

The bartender smiled tightly. 'Not a thing, Marshal.'

'Don't gimme that! They's somethin' goin' on. I jist seen Ike Canfield come out staggerin'. He fell down twice gettin' acrost the street, then dunked 'is head in the horse-trough. Now what's goin' on?'

'Ike just tried to bully the wrong man, that's all Marshal.'

'Somebody stood up to Ike?'

'I guess you could say that. Ike sorta lay down on the floor and slept a bit, anyway '

'You tellin' me thet somebody knocked Ike out?'

'One punch, Marshal.'

'Who?'

The bartender looked at Levi. 'You want me to tell 'im?'

'Prob'ly ought to,' Levi said. 'He ain't likely to figure much out unless someone tells 'im. Use real small words, and talk slow.'

Several voices laughed, but chopped the laughter off short when the marshal whirled to glare at them. He turned back to Levi.

'You hit Ike?'

Levi's patience hit its end.

'You got a problem with that, Marshal? Is he some pet o' yours that you need to take care of?'

Deathly silence erupted in the room again. The marshal blinked several times, obviously trying to figure out his best course of action. He tried bluster.

'Listen, Hill. I don't care who you are er who you work fer. You ain't welcome in this town. Ya got two choices. You kin git outa town, or I'll lock ya up.'

Levi stepped away from the bar. His hand dropped to an inch from his gun butt. The tight rein of restraint he had kept on his anger slipped a notch. He took a step toward the blustering marshal.

'Is that a fact? And what charge do you plan to dream up to justify that, Marshal? Do you think you can just make up your own laws? If you think you're man enough to arrest me on some trumped-up charge, you go right ahead. But if you raise the barrel of that shotgun two inches I'll kill you before it gets to three inches. I've listened to your asinine bluster and dither ever since I rode into this town, and the sooner I'm gone from here the better I'll like it. But neither you nor any other two-bit blowhard is going to run me out of town until I've finished the job I came here to do. I am a Deputy United States Marshal, and I do have both the authority and the ability to take that tin badge off of your puffed-up chest and stuff it in your big mouth if I need to.'

The marshal blinked several times in the deathly silence that followed Levi's tirade. He tried desperately to regain some of his bluster.

'Listen, Hill, this town don't need your highfalutin words and bigshot authority an' almighty intelligence—'

'This town doesn't need your stupidity and lazy insolence either, Marshal. Now get out of here and go hide in your office before I lose my temper. I've had all of you I can stomach for one day. I've never shot but one lawman in my life, but I swear it'll be two if I see you again this day.'

The marshal tried to meet the steel of his gaze for a moment, then gave up the effort.

'You jist steer clear o' me, Hill,' he said as he

headed for the door. Over his shoulder, on the way out he yelled: 'You jist may find ya've bit off more'n ya kin chew if'n ya try to tangle with the likes o' me.'

Levi turned back to his beer. The bartender, standing straight across the bar from him, spoke.

'Well, that's two o' the people I'd most like to see somebody take down a peg or two. Both in one day. Not bad. Next beer's on me. You watch your back, though.'

'I kinda got a habit o' that. Which one'll be behind me?'

'It won't be Ike. He'll most likely be comin' after you, once his head stops spinnin'. But it won't be from behind. He's a bully, but mostly because nobody can stand up to him. He's not a coward. The marshal, on the other hand . . .'

'Thanks. That's sorta the way I had it figured.'

He walked out of the saloon, looking carefully up and down the street before stepping out from the shadow of the building. He almost hoped he'd see the marshal coming after him. Or Ike. Either one. It didn't matter. Or to have one of those nicey-nice ladies of Cheerful scold him for being a gunman. Right now he'd love to grab one of them sniffing, huffing old bags and turn her bottom side up and paddle her behind.

He shook his head, trying to quell the rotten mood. He needed to go talk to Myra. She always put him in a better mood. He needed to do a lot more than just talk to Myra. That'd really help his mood. He shook his head, scolding himself.

'Watch it, Levi. You've never been a man who used

51

CHAPTER 6

'I was married once. That's enough.'

Levi studied Myra's face carefully.

'Not a good marriage?'

Her eyes clouded briefly.

'It was a great marriage. We were as perfectly suited to each other as two people can be, I think.'

'Then why wouldn't you want it again?'

He couldn't remember another time when she'd seemed at a loss for words. It took her several minutes to answer, as she busied herself straightening clothes on the shelf of the store. Trying to lighten the mood that he had so obviously darkened, Levi offered:

'You couldn't likely come up with that sort of a name twice.'

She giggled unexpectedly. 'Funderburke? You don't like my name?'

'Oh, I like it fine. It brings half a dozen quips to mind every time I hear it. I'd just hate to have to wear it.'

'I'm sure I've heard every quip you've thought of,

53

at least a dozen times,' she rued. 'Hansel thought about changing it a lot of times.'

'Hansel Funderburke. I can see why he would. Why didn't he? Lots of folks out here wear a name they just picked out of the blue. Nobody ever does know what name they started out with.'

'That's true. But he was proud of his parents and his grandparents. He felt that changing his name, just to get away from a lot of lame jokes, would be betraying his legacy from them.'

'Well, there's something to that, I guess. But that doesn't explain why you'd never want to get married again.'

She sighed. 'Quite a few reasons, really. I doubt another marriage would ever be as good as that one. We were just so totally open with each other, and thought the same things at the same time, and felt the same about almost everything – it was almost like being married to a fantasy I'd created in my mind of the perfect husband. I think any other marriage would constantly disappoint me in a hundred small ways.'

'Might even be better in some ways, though.'

'Maybe,' she admitted, 'but I doubt it. Then there's the selfish side of me.'

'What do you mean?'

'Well, I'm single. I can do as I please. I don't have to think about pleasing a husband. I don't have to wonder if he likes how I fix my hair, or what I wear. If I don't feel like talking, I don't have to talk. If I take a notion to go for a ride, I don't have to tell anyone where I'm going or when I'm going to be back. If I want to sing and dance naked around the front room, I don't have to wonder what anyone else thinks.'

'Now that'd be a sight to behold. You do that often?'

Her eyes danced. 'That's for you to wonder, Mr Hill. I'll give you those fantasies to keep you company on lonely nights around your camp-fire.'

'They just might do that, too,' he admitted. 'Of course, it'd be a shame to have them just be fantasies. Memories make a lot better company than wishes.'

'Levi Hill! Are you offering me a proposition?'

'Well, the thought crossed my mind.'

She struck a melodramatic pose, with the back of her hand pressed against her forehead, her head tilted back.

'Oh, not tonight, dear. I have a terrible headache.'

'Just my luck,' he lamented. 'What happened to Hansel? If you don't mind my asking.'

Her mood sobered instantly. A distant look clouded her eyes.

'You aren't very seductive, are you? Just when you had me thinking about things I shouldn't think about, you bring me back to earth.'

'Sorry.' He truly was sorry, too. He didn't know what had prompted him to break the mood that was obviously building by throwing in that question.

She sighed. 'I found him after a terrible storm. We had a small ranch up north a ways. He went out to make sure the cows had found shelter, with a big storm coming in. He never made it back to the house. He was frozen to death, less than two hundred yards from the door.'

'I'm sorry,' he said again. 'Couldn't quite make it back, huh?'

Her face turned hard. 'He would have, by himself.'

'What do you mean?'

'Someone killed him.'

'Killed him?'

She nodded. 'There was a knot over one ear. The marshal just said he froze to death, and I suppose he did. But I saw the knot over his ear when I found him. I went out at first light, looking for him. I saw one hand sticking out of the snow, where it had drifted. Otherwise, I wouldn't have found him until the snow melted. He was frozen stiff as a board. But there was a big knot over his right ear. Someone knocked him out, and left him to freeze to death.'

'Didn't you tell the marshal?'

She shrugged. 'Oh, sure. I told everyone I could get to listen. But they all said he must have fallen and hit his head on something. Tripped on something under the snow, they said. Folks do that all the time. Just one of those freak things. But he didn't. I know he was murdered. Of course, the snow covered up any tracks, so nobody could tell whether there had been anyone else there.'

'Any idea who might've wanted to kill him?'

'That's why nobody would even listen to me. He didn't have an enemy in the world. He'd have given the shirt off his back to anyone who needed it. He never turned a range bum away without a square meal. He was always ready to help anyone out who needed a hand. He just liked people, and everyone in the country liked him. It didn't make any sense at all.'

'So what makes you so sure it wasn't just an accident?'

She shrugged. 'Woman's intuition, maybe. And I looked, after the snow melted. There just wasn't anything anywhere near where he froze that he could have hit his head on. And how would he hit the side of his head, above the ear, falling down?'

'His horse wouldn't have kicked him, maybe?'

She shook her head. 'He shouldn't have even been off his horse, there. There was no fence, no gate, no cattle there. He was just on his way home. The barn door wasn't latched. The horse came on home and went in the barn. He was still standing there, in the barn, with the saddle still on, the next morning.'

'So you think someone knocked him out of the saddle?'

'Probably not. It seemed more like he must have gotten off his horse to talk to someone. Then when he went to get back on his horse, whoever it was hit him with a gun barrel or something.'

'If someone wanted to kill him, why didn't he just shoot him?'

'To make it look like an accident.'

Levi thought about it for a long moment, turning over the revelations in his mind. He had to admit, Myra's logic was compelling. They were interrupted by a couple entering the store.

'Hi, Ben. Hi, Lola,' Myra greeted. 'I thought you were about due to be coming in. Haven't seen you for a couple weeks at least.'

'I've been getting cabin fever,' Lola lamented. 'I eventually told Ben if he didn't get me to town for a day or two I was going to go stark raving mad.'

'I don't understand why she needs to come to town,' Ben teased. 'She has me to talk to out at the place. What could be better than that?'

'Because I already know every joke you tell by heart,' Lola rejoined. 'Besides, you spend more time talking to the cows than you do to me.'

'They never argue with me,' Ben said.

'Neither do I. I just tell you when you're wrong.'

'But I'm never wrong.'

A new voice entered the conversation. 'Now there's something every wife needs to know and understand. Her husband is never wrong.'

As they all turned to look at the newcomer, the dapper young gambler grinned broadly. 'Now if you could teach me how to convince the little lady of that, I might, myself, consider matrimony.'

Lola's chin lifted. 'If you knew how to make a lady admit such a thing as that, you wouldn't be fit for matrimony.'

'Ah, then, perhaps my father was right.'

'And what did your father say about the subject, Mr Bassett?'

With only a hint of a wry smile playing about the corners of his mouth, the gambler said:

'My father told me in the wisdom of his years, that any man who says he is the boss of his own household will probably lie about other things too.'

They all laughed together. Lola lifted her chin

impudently at her husband.

'See, dear? Now here is a smart man. He knows enough to let a lady be right, even if she isn't.'

The tiniest of flashes in the depths of his eyes was masked by an easy smile on Ben's lips.

'Ah, but you must consider, my dear, the man is single. He hasn't experienced the joys of always being wrong at first hand.'

The gambler, still smiling, turned to Myra.

'Myra, my dear, I wonder if you would be so good as to sell me a new shirt that will be a better choice of fabric and color than I might be expected to make on my own.'

'Of course,' Myra agreed. 'A woman's touch is essential to keeping you the best dressed man in Cheerful.'

'It's only your flawless advice on my accouterments that keeps me the most sought-after bachelor in the region. How can I deny it.'

Everyone laughed easily at the remark, but Levi had the distinct feeling that Ben's laughter was only on the surface. He noticed the rancher move closer to his pretty young wife and slide a hand along her arm.

'Shall we pick out the things you wanted, Lola?'

'Sure,' she agreed.

As Levi looked on, the gambler was paying for his new shirt, still tossing lighthearted banter back and forth with the rancher and his wife. Most of it, he noticed, was directed to Lola. Only when they were almost ready to leave did Myra notice the neglected customer.

'Oh, I'm sorry!' She approached the young cowboy whom Levi had verbally clashed with. 'I didn't even see you come in, Bucky. Can I help you with something?'

'Aw, I guess I jist need some new britches,' the young man said. 'I ain't in no hurry.'

'Are you sure? You don't mind waiting? I'm almost finished.'

'Thet's fine.'

When Ben and Lola left, and then the gambler had followed a few minutes later, she waited on the cowboy.

'Thet gambler's sure took a shine to thet lady. Miss Lola, I mean,' Bucky remarked.

Myra's eyebrows lifted. 'Oh, he just talks to everyone like that.'

Bucky's lips were drawn tightly. 'I don't think her husband liked it none.'

'Ben? Oh, he doesn't mind. He's pretty proud of Lola. She's quite a bit younger than he is.'

The cowhand nodded, his frown unaffected.

'He's way too old fer her all right. That's fer sure.'

She took the young man's money, and forgot him nearly as soon as he was out the door. Levi had watched him long enough to be sure he had no intention of resuming their previous unpleasantries, then paid little more attention to him. Bucky never acknowledged Levi's presence in any way, nor gave any indication of remembering their previous encounter.

As soon as Myra was alone with him, Levi spoke.

'Would you mind fillin' me in on who all them

60

folks are? Other'n Art Bassett. I've seen him hangin' out at the Dusty Soul, lookin' fer cowhands to relieve of their money.'

'He's really a pleasant person, though,' Myra defended. 'Even if he is a gambler. I think he's as honest as a gambler can be. Plays by the rules. But he is good. He doesn't lose much of the time. The couple is Ben and Lola Jordan. They have a ranch over east about three miles. They're a lot of fun to wait on. Always poking fun at each other. I think they have a great marriage, even if he is older.'

'The other cowpoke didn't seem so sure of that. Bucky Denton. Right? Where's he from?'

Her eyes were suddenly distant. 'You know, I'm not sure I've ever heard him say. I think he rides for the Rafter M. I'm not even sure of that, though. He's one of those ranch hands who are just there. He never causes any trouble or gets drunk and starts fights, so I've just never really paid any attention. Actually, I've never liked him enough to pay attention, I guess. He's one of those people who seem to think everyone else is doing something wrong. Really serious all the time. Judgmental. That's the word. He is one very judgmental young man.'

Levi dismissed Bucky from his mind, as their conversation turned to others living in the valley. He came back again to Ben and Lola Jordan.

'That Jordan couple still seems a bit odd to me. That's a big age difference.'

'Not that unusual though,' Myra argued. 'At least when it's in that direction. It's more unusual the other way.'

'What other way?'

'If the woman's older. For some reason nobody thinks a young man ought to ever fall in love with an older woman, but a young woman can fall in love with an older man and that's just fine.'

'Well, you have to admit, it doesn't happen that often.'

'But it does happen. Even around here.'

'It does?'

'Sure. How about the McCallums?'

'What about the McCallums. I've never heard of them.'

'Oh. I guess I didn't mention them, and you wouldn't have met them, I don't suppose. They have a ranch in the same general direction as Ben and Lola. About ten miles from their place, I suppose. Maybe less. Anyway, Sean McCallum is a young, red-headed, freckle-faced Irish cowboy who's probably twenty years old and looks all of fifteen. Maria is a really beautiful Mexican woman, but she has to be in her mid-thirties at least. She looks a little hard around the mouth, and around her eyes, but when she smiles she lights up a place. And she does have a young woman's figure.'

'And they're married?'

'Uh huh. And she's at least fifteen years older than him. It's almost funny to watch them. He doesn't just love that woman, he worships her. He waits on her like she's a queen. Even when they're in town, he can't take his eyes off of her for five minutes. Most men go over to the Dusty Soul to have a drink or two while their wives shop. Not Sean. He doesn't leave her side for a minute. I sometimes wonder how he leaves her home alone long enough to get the ranch work done.'

'Plumb smitten with her, huh? What does she see in him?'

Myra shrugged. 'I suppose she's in love, too. That happens, you know. And she sure couldn't find anyone that'd be any better to her. I've always had the suspicion that there's something in her past, though.'

'Something like what?'

She shrugged again. 'I have no idea. Just a woman's intuition. Just a feeling that there's something there that she doesn't talk about. Maybe something that Sean took her away from, or something she doesn't want him or anyone else to know.'

'Most folks out here have a past of some kind. Seems strange, anyway.'

The two couples stuck in his mind. 'Oughta put both couples in a gunny-sack an' shake 'em up, an' maybe they'd come out more evenly matched.'

Myra giggled. 'It's a good thing you don't get to make the matches for folks.'

He had to agree. He couldn't even come up with one for himself.

CHAPTER 7

Water cascaded in a white plume nearly sixty feet down the sheer rock face. Its roar filled the clearing. The large pool at the bottom, worn deep by years of the plummeting water, was certain to be filled with hungry trout. They sat their horses, side by side, drinking in the thundering beauty of Thompson Falls. It was everything she had said it was. The oppressive pounding of the din against his ears filled him with a sense of dark foreboding. The hair on the back of his neck tingled as it stirred.

The dog stood close beside the horse, almost against its front leg. His tail was tucked tightly between his legs. His ears drooped. His soft whine was lost in the tumult, but it was evident he was as disquieted by the thundering rumble of the falls as his master.

Myra reined her horse around and rode close beside him. She spoke close to his ear, to be heard above the roar of the falls.

'We could eat our lunch over there in that nice patch of grass,' she said.

Levi shook his head. He leaned close to her ear, that she might hear his reply. The smell of her hair and just a whisper of perfume filled him with a sudden sense of longing. He frowned against it.

'Too noisy,' he said. 'We can't talk. Besides, I get nervous when I can't hear anything.'

She nodded. Lifting the reins she nudged her horse downstream. He followed, his nerves screaming in protest. His eyes darted everywhere, peering into the denseness of the forest, scanning the top of the cliff by the falls, probing the banks of the stream ahead.

As they rode along the babbling merriment of the stream, the roar of the falls faded into the background. By half a mile they could barely hear it. A level park, speckled with wild flowers, carpeted with thick grass, reached back into the forest, opening a space of several acres. Brush growing thick along the bank of the stream muffled even the sound of its babbling.

'How's this?' Myra asked.

'A whole lot better than by the falls. That much noise scares me to death. Mostly because I couldn't hear anyone coming, I suppose.'

'Just the effect of the noise itself does that,' she agreed. 'It's intimidatmg.'

'It's all of that.'

'I tried to stand under it once.'

'What? The water?'

'Uh huh. I thought it would be the ultimate thrill to let the water cascade over me. There's a little ledge at the bottom, where you can walk behind the falls. I

65

walked out there, and then stuck my hand out into the water.'

'And it didn't tear your arm off?'

'It almost did,' she admitted. 'I had no idea water would feel like that when it had fallen that far. It felt like some giant hand just grabbed hold of me. It jerked me right off the ledge, and shoved me down into that deep pool under it. It felt like an elephant had fallen on me.'

'Lucky you didn't drown.'

'Pure luck, I think. The current comes back up as fast as it goes down, and it threw me up to the surface, out from under the falls itself. I couldn't have stayed under water another second by that time, though. As it was, I was barely able to get to shore. The next day my whole arm, my shoulders and back, and even the backs of my legs were all black and blue. I looked like I'd been beaten.'

'You had. Water is powerful stuff. You're lucky you didn't drown.'

'I think you said that already. Anyway, I didn't. I got over the soreness. It's nice and quiet here. Does this spot suit your nerves better?'

'This is just about as perfect a spot as God could make,' Levi enthused. 'You were right. This is a beautiful country.'

'I told you you'd like it up here.'

'It's a good climb getting here, too. I'm hungry enough to catch a trout and eat it raw.'

'Why are you so hungry? Your horse did all the climbing,' she teased.

'Yeah, but I had to help him. I was pushing on this

saddle horn to help him up every hill.'

She laughed merrily. 'Oh, I'm sure that was a big help.'

'Yeah, I was sort of standing in my stirrups, too, so my weight wouldn't be as heavy in the saddle.'

'I'm surprised he didn't almost float up here, with all that help.'

A cottontail rabbit burst from a clump of brush.

'Get 'im, Curly,' Levi said.

Instantly the dog that flanked them burst into a dead run. The rabbit disappeared into the brush and trees, darting first one way then another, with the dog close on its heels. They sat their horses in silence, listening to the two crashing through brush and branches. Then there was silence.

'Did he get him?'

'I don't know. We'll find out afore long.'

They didn't have long to wait. In little more than a minute the dog appeared at the edge of the trees, the rabbit dangling from his mouth.

'Well, it looks like Curly's got his lunch,' Levi observed. 'Now we don't have to share any of ours with him.'

The dog lay down in the tall grass and began to tear at the warmth of the fresh meat. They hobbled their horses, loosened the cinches, and removed the bridles to allow the animals to eat of the lush offering of the Edenic profusion.

The conversation continued about everything and nothing as she spread out their lunch and they ate. Time slid past as they forgot, for a little while, everything except each other. The shadows of the forest moved to the other side of the trees, as the sun moved beyond its zenith. Too soon to suit Myra, Levi's gaze became distant and his attention began to waver.

'I'm beginning to feel downright ugly all of a sudden,' she protested, teasingly. 'Here we are, up here a dozen miles from anything, in a perfectly romantic spot, and I just can't keep your mind off of trying to solve a crime.'

'Oh. Sorry,' he apologized. 'Yeah, you're right. My mind was wandering. I guess I'm not being very good company.'

'On the contrary, I'm delighted. It's been a long time since I've dared to get clear away from town with anybody like this. It's really nice to find some-one I can both talk to and trust.'

'Yeah, well, don't push it too far. You don't know me very well.'

'Well enough to know I like what I've found so far. Do you want to go back?'

'No, but I 'spect we should. No telling whose gotten themselves killed since we've been gone.'

'Our situation in Cheerful is really bothering you, isn't it.'

'Seems to be. Maybe it's because none of it makes any sense. The only thing the ones that've been killed have in common is that they didn't have an enemy in the world. Usually it's a matter of sorting out all the folks who had a reason to kill someone, and figure out which one of the bunch that hated 'im did it. Here there just isn't anybody to sort out. It makes no sense.'

'I know. I've struggled with that ever since Hansel was killed. In all that time, I haven't come up with a single possibility.'

'Maybe I'll ride out and talk with Cap'n Renfro.'

'Who?'

'Jesse Renfro.'

'Oh. Why did you call him "captain"?'

'He used to be a captain with the Texas Rangers.'

'Jesse did? I didn't know that.'

'Neither does anyone else around, I don't think. He doesn't want it known, either, by the way. If it isn't noised around, there's less chance of someone showing up to settle some old score. He retired from the Rangers. Went to ranchin'.'

'And you think he might know something?'

Levi shrugged. 'Hard to tell. He's been around a long time, seen a lot of things. He might have some ideas, at least. If he's got one good idea, that's one more than I've got.'

The light mood of the day and the easy, light-hearted conversation was gone. The sense of connection between them moved back, as both allowed their own thoughts to isolate them from one another. The ride back to town was punctuated with only occasional conversation. When they arrived back at her house, he unsaddled her horse and rubbed him down while she filled the feed-box with oats. Then he took his own horse back to the livery barn.

He stepped out of the livery barn to find Ike Canfield standing in the middle of the street, waiting for him. His feet were planted about two feet apart. He leaned forward, his shoulders pointed toward

Levi. His fists clenched and unclenched at his sides.

'Been waitin' fer you, Hill,' he rumbled. 'You ain't gonna sucker-punch me this time.'

'It's Sunday, Ike,' Levi reminded him.

'Don't make no difference to me. I got a Sunday punch er two that been itchin' fer you.'

The two eyed each other warily for several seconds, then Ike rushed forward, sending a wild haymaker looping toward Levi's head.

Levi easily stepped out of the way, letting it whistle past, sending a short right of his own toward the big man's ear. To Levi's surprise Ike swatted it away just as easily and sent a quick left into Levi's wind. Levi grunted in surprise and backed up quickly. In spite of his size and brutishness, this guy was quick!

Levi hastily sidestepped and ducked four swift blows, any one of which would have rocked him. He jabbed Ike's nose hard twice with his left, slipping aside quickly enough from the answering right that came over the jabs and barely grazed his ear. Even so, it stung like frostbite on a winter day. He followed over the top of Ike's right with a hard left hook that connected with Ike's right cheek.

Without slowing, Levi whirled away in a complete circle, his outside leg whipping high. The heel of his boot connected with the side of Ike's head with a thud.

The big man staggered half a step, shook his head, and bored back in on Levi. Levi met him with a straight right to the mouth, then a quick chop into his belly. To his surprise he took three solid blows from Ike while he was doing so, two to the left side of his head and one to the right.

He spun away again and warily circled the big man. They swung and feinted, parried and counter-punched. Each gave as good as he received. They were both unaware of the shouts that rang out up and down the street of the excited crowd that assembled to watch the fight everyone had known must come, sooner or later. If he had noticed her, Levi would have thought the one most out of place was Myra, arms folded across her chest, watching with obvious but silent concern.

They fought until Levi's arms felt like leaden weights. Throwing caution to the winds, Ike abruptly sprang at him, swinging with both fists. Levi backed away three steps, then stepped into a straight left aimed at Ike's chin.

Ike jerked his head aside, and took only a glancing blow that opened a cut along his jaw. Levi followed instantly with four swift, chopping blows to the brow above both of Ike's eyes. Instantly blood began pouring from the opened cuts, running down into his eyes.

Ike swiped at the blood, trying to clear his vision. It was, at last, the opening Levi needed. He planted his feet and sent a series of blows into Ike's face, followed with four solid body punches, stepped back half a step, then forward, bringing the weight of his body and the last vestiges of his remaining strength into a right hook that connected solidly with Ike's jaw. Levi felt the bone crunch and break beneath his fist.

He stepped away. Ike dropped to his knees.

'Better kick 'im while you can,' somebody shouted.

'You let 'im get back up, you won't get another chance,' another agreed.

'He ain't gonna get up,' a third voice disagreed.

'I got a buck says he does.'

'You're on.'

'I got two says he's done.'

Aware for the first time of the crowd that had assembled to watch, Levi backed away, watching the big man. Ike toppled slowly forward, burying his face in the dirt of the street. His knees kicked back spasmodically, leaving him stretched face down, unmoving.

Acting on instinct, Levi stepped forward, grabbed Ike by the hair, and turned his head to the side, allowing him to breathe.

The voices of the crowd erupted in an excited hubbub from which no individual words could be understood. Maybe it was the buzzing roar in his ears that made it difficult to understand.

'You better come over to the house and let me get you cleaned up,' said a voice at his elbow. 'You look like you got trampled in a stampede.'

Levi shook his head, trying to rid himself of the sound of Thompson Falls that seemed to be pounding in his ears. It was a futile effort.

'He musta clipped me a time or two,' he muttered.

'More than a time or two,' Myra corrected him. Her voice was low enough for only him to hear her. 'You two fought like a couple mad old bulls. If I don't get your hands to soaking in salts right away, they're going to get too stiff for you to handle your guns. Now take my arm and act like you're guiding me, and let me help you to the house.'

Numbly, fighting against the dizziness and weariness that followed the ebbing of his adrenaline, he complied. He thought the charade of pretending he was doing the leading must be comically obvious, until he heard a voice speak up from the excited crowd.

'Look at that, would ya! Jist takes 'er arm an' walks off like 'e ain't even been in a fight.'

He certainly knew he'd been in a fight. He knew he'd be very much more aware of it by morning.

CHAPTER 8

Flexing his hands still hurt. Not seriously. Just enough to remind him to keep flexing them every little while. They could still stiffen enough to slow his draw significantly. That could be fatal.

With his back to the wall he studied the patrons of the Dusty Soul. There were only two working girls, whose presence gave the place its only feminine flavor. He watched them circulate among the customers, hollow smiles pasted to their tired mouths. He thought suddenly how terribly lonely they must be. No woman to talk with except the other whore who worked that establishment. The other women of the town certainly wouldn't be caught dead speaking to one of them. Their relationship with the customers was exactly that – take care of the customer and move on to the next. They probably went for years without talking to anyone who really cared what they felt, or thought, or longed for. Nobody ever wondered whose little girl they used to be, or whether they still ran to daddy's arms in their dreams. To be that utterly alone in the middle of a constant flow of people must be the loneliest existence in the world.

Except a range detective. Gunman. Outcast. Pariah. Well, at least Myra enjoyed his company. They were drawn to each other like two starving dogs to a beef roast. He almost chuckled at the thought.

The westering sun showed dimly through the impossibly dirty window, and made a bright yellow rectangle inside the door on the sawdust floor. Flies buzzed and crawled in that square of light, giving a constant illusion of motion to the sawdust.

The back door of the saloon burst open, slamming against the wall with a loud bang. Unaware he had even drawn, Levi held his .45 trained on the young man who rushed in.

'Fred!' he yelled at the bartender. 'Fred! Someone went an' kilt Art!'

The bartender's eyes darted to Levi, then back to the young intruder.

'Art Bassett?'

'Yeah! He's deader'n a doornail, too.'

'Where?'

'Out back. He's out in the weeds.'

'Did you see him get killed?' Levi interjected.

The young man's eyes swivelled to Levi.

'Oh, no! I jist pertneart tripped on 'im, that there's how I come to find 'im.'

'Well, let's go take a look,' Levi said, standing and holstering his gun. 'Show me.'

The young man bobbed his head up and down like a cork with a bluegill taking the bait.

'Sure, mister. I'll show ya. Y'll see. He's deader'n a

doornail all right.'

'You sure he's not just deader'n a mackerel?'

'Huh? What's a mackerel?'

'Never mind. Show him to me.'

'Oh. Yeah. Sure. He's out this way.'

Vaguely aware of at least half a dozen people trailing out after them, Levi followed the excited youth. Fifty feet from the back door, face down in tall weeds and grass, the body of the gambler lay stretched full length. The handle and about two inches of the blade of a large knife protruded from his back.

Well-placed knife, Levi noted silently. *Between the ribs, probably cut his heart completely in two. He'd have died almost instantly. Didn't even have time to turn around to see who killed him.*

'See,' the youth asserted. 'It's jist like I said. Deader'n a doornail. Plumb stone-cold dead. Stiffer'n a board.'

Levi felt the body below the arm, along the side. There was no hint of warmth left. He had to have been dead several hours. He turned to Fred, the bartender, standing with the circle of the curious.

'He been in the saloon today?'

Fred shook his head. 'Nope. He went home kinda early last night. Wasn't much action fer 'im to make anything off of. Hadn't seen 'im since.'

'Anyone lose a bunch of money last night?'

Fred shrugged. 'Not to notice. He didn't play much. Four or five of 'em played cards for a couple hours. Nobody complained about losin'.'

'Anyone leave with him?'

'Not that I noticed. No. No, there wasn't. He

always came in and out the back door. Not many other folks do. Nobody else went out that way.'

'Anyone leave about the same time by the front door?'

He shrugged again. 'Not that I took notice of. Cowboys sorta come an' go. Townsfolk too. Mighta been someone left about the same time, but I didn't take no note of it.'

Levi studied the knife-handle. He turned his head, addressing the interested arc of faces that peered back.

'Anyone recognize the knife?'

One young man cleared his throat. He thrust his hand up, like a child offering an answer in school.

'Uh, yeah.'

'Who're you?'

'Uh, Jimmy Malone. I work for the blacksmith.'

'You know that knife?'

'Uh, well, I think so. Maybe, I mean.'

'Well, who do you maybe think it might belong to?'

'Uh, well, it sorta looks like the butcher-knife Sally Strotheim uses.'

'Who's she?'

'Uh, Sally's a he. Name's Sally, but he's a he.'

'OK. Who's he?'

'Uh, well, he's the cook, over at the Grubline.'

Nearly a dozen pairs of eyes the crowd had grown to turned in unison to look toward the back of the Grubline Café, half a block down the street from the Dusty Soul. 'You sure of that?'

'Uh, well, no. Not positive, er nothin'. Just looks

like it. That's all. It's got a sort of a odd handle, an' all. Sally, he made the handle himself, I think. Out of a hunk of wood.'

Levi resisted the urge to say: *Yup. It sure is wood, all right.* He had the feeling the young man would answer as if it were the wisest thing he'd heard said all day.

He walked over to the dead gambler's body. He grasped the knife-handle. With effort he pulled it from the lifeless body. Blood was dried almost black where it was at the surface of the flesh, but clung bright red to the rest of the blade. Kneeling on one knee, Levi wiped the blade as clean as he could on the grass and weeds. He stood. He addressed the bartender.

'Fred, would you mind sendin' someone to inform the fearless marshal that this one is well within his jurisdiction?'

'Sure thing. Anything else you want me to tell 'im?'

'Well, you might tell 'im it appears the man's dead. Tell 'im I took the knife out of him and he didn't yell, anyway. I'm going to go have a talk with Sally. You sure that's a man's name?'

Fred's eyes twinkled, but Levi was unsure whether because of his sarcasm or the oddity of the name.

'I'm plumb sure. He don't take too kindly to folks makin' fun of it, neither. He says his pa's name was Dorothy an' his brother's name is Joyce. He says all them names is men's names where his family come from.'

'Is that so?'

'So he says. Nobody gives him no trouble over it, neither.'

'Why's that?'

Fred shrugged. 'He's the only one in town Ike Canfield gives room to. Well, 'cept you nowadays, I 'spect.'

Levi turned the information over in his mind.

'He have any doin's with Bassett?'

'Not that I know of. He played cards with 'im, time to time. Most o' the guys did. Art, he was an odd sort o' gambler, though. Good natured sort. Seemed plumb honest, even if he was a gambler. Don't know of nobody ever accusin' 'im o' cheatin'. That's sorta odd, ya know, fer a gambler. Most everybody thinks they cheat when they lose to 'em. Art didn't seem to wanta make a big hunk o' money. Just liked ta gamble, an' did well enough at it ta get by.'

'Not an enemy in the world,' Levi muttered.

'What?'

'Nothin'.' He addressed the small crowd. 'You fellas'd just as well go back inside. I'm sure the marshal will have a few questions to ask you, along with askin' volunteers to haul Art over to the undertaker.'

He walked away as the group slowly drifted back toward the Dusty Soul, talking excitedly among themselves.

A wave of heat, along with the smell of grease and food and soap mixed together assailed his nostrils as he stepped in the open back door of the Grubline Café. With his back to the door, a large man with hair so blond it was almost white hunched over a butcher-block. Nobody else seemed to be in the kitchen.

'Sally Strotheim?'

The man stood up straight and turned to face him. His broad face had an open quality that made his bright-blue eyes look like windows into open sky.

'Yah! I am Sally.'

As he spoke, he looked Levi up and down. His gaze fell on the knife in Levi's hand. His eyes lit up as if sparks from a flint had landed on gunpowder.

'My knife! My Yimminy, you found my knife. I haf looked eferywhere for dat. Vere haf you found it?'

Levi studied his face carefully as he responded.

'I found it stickin' out of a fella's back.'

Sally's eyes darted to his, then back to the knife, back to his, then stuck to the ring of black-dried blood that hadn't wiped off on the weeds. He swallowed visibly.

'Mine knife hast killed a man?'

Instead of answering, Levi said: 'When was the last you saw your knife?'

'Oof da! I used it yesterday. But dis morning, ven I haf come in to start vith da breakfast tings, it is not dere.'

'Where do you keep it?'

Sally waved toward a rack of knives attached to the side of the meat-block. He didn't speak.

'It was put away last night?'

'Yah. Alvays I sharpen dem ven I am done for da day, and put dem avay dere.'

'Do you lock up at night?'

'Oof da! Vy vould ve lock tings?'

Levi nodded. 'So somebody must've come in after

you closed, or before you got here this morning, and took it?'

Sally shrugged. 'I vas not here dis morning.'

'Where'd you go after you closed up last night?'

'I vent ofer to der Dusty Soul for a beer.'

'Play cards?'

'Yah. For a vile.'

'Who with?'

'Vel, mit Artur, of course. Und tree or four cowboys.'

'Do you remember who?'

Sally shrugged again. He swiped a hand across the balding front of his head, pushing the white-blond hair back from the even whiter skin of his high fore-head.

'Not really. Vel, der vas der gangly fellow vat used to vork at der Box-tree . . .'

'Spider?'

'Yah. Das ist vat his name ist. Und der qviet vun.'

'Quiet one?'

'Yah. Der ist vun young cowboy dat ist a tinker. He isn't saying notting, very much. Alvays, he ist tinking.'

'Do you know his name?'

He shrugged again. 'No, I don't tink I know it. Vun day ve vill.'

'Oh? Why do you say that?'

'Because he ist a tinker. He isn't talking. He ist alvays tinking. Dem dat is doing tinking all the time, someday, wen dey gets der tinkings all figured out, den dey amounts to sometings. Den ve all remember der names, and ve say: "Oh, I knowed him wen he vas yust a young fellow".'

'And it was just the three of you?'

'No. Der vas vun otter fellow, but I don't remember who it vas.'

'Who won?'

'Vel, I von so long as I could keep Artur playing stud. Mit fife-card stud, I can beat him, some of der time. Most of der time, maybe. Mit fife-card draw, Art ist too good. I tink I vas maybe fifty cents or a dollar ahead wen ve svitched to draw. Den I lost mine dollar and anotter beside.'

'Did anyone else lose much?'

Sally shrugged again. 'Not fery much. Not enough dat I notice. Who ist der man dat vas killed?'

'It was Art.'

'Artur? No! He vas killed? Vere? How did it happened?'

'Someone stabbed him from behind with your knife. Slipped it between his ribs, all the way in.'

'Ach! Ach Sule Gud! Mit mine knife dey haf killed Artur! Who hast done dis ting?'

It was Levi's turn to shrug.

'I don't know. It had to be someone who knew you kept your knives here, though. Did anyone leave just a while ahead of Art?'

Sally shrugged in an almost comic repetition of Levi's imitation of him.

'I vas goned before Artur left.'

'So someone could have come over here, gotten your knife, then waited for Art to come out the back door, either to relieve himself out in the weeds or go home. Must've been relievin' himself, come to think about it, bein' out there where he was.'

He handed Sally the knife. The big man took it, acting almost as if he thought it might bite him. Without saying anything more, Levi turned and walked out.

CHAPTER 9

'I've learned to make do, I guess, but land sakes, it's hard.'

Levi eyed the forty-something ranch woman.

'I'm sure it is. It's good that your foreman stayed on, though.'

Charolette Walters nodded her agreement, watching him over the rim of her coffee-cup.

'I couldn't have made it without him. Luther always took care of everything except the house and the kids. I didn't have any least idea how to run a ranch.'

'It must've been a real shock.'

She nodded again, her eyes clouding.

'It might have been easier if I'd had some idea it was coming.'

'No idea at all who might have wanted to kill him?'

She shook her head, setting the coffee-cup down but still holding it with both hands wrapped around it. Her eyes made their habitual circle around her spotless kitchen, then went back to stare into the dark liquid in the cup.

'Not even a slim one. The day before he was killed, I was thinking about how lucky I was to have a husband whom everyone in the country liked so much. We'd been to town. We talked to Ben and Lola in the mercantile store for over an hour. Luther loved to tease Lola. She'd act like she was all embarrassed and shy, but you could tell she was really enjoying it. I think we must have visited with over a dozen people, all told, before we left for home. And every one of them acted like they just wished we could stay and visit all day. And Lord knows it's never been me that folks have liked to talk to. It's always been Luther. He just loved to talk, and loved to listen just as much. That's my downfall. I like to talk all right, I just forget to listen to anybody else. Not Luther. He knew about everything there was to know about everyone in the country, but he never talked about folks. Nobody ever knew he knew all the things he knew, 'cause he'd just talk and talk, and listen and listen, but never say a blessed thing that anyone didn't want known. Land sakes, that man was a gem. And now here I am running this ranch by myself without him. Who'd have ever dreamed of such a thing.'

Levi frowned, wedging a thought into the closed joints of her words.

'You say Luther spent a while talking with Lola the day before he was killed?'

'Oh, Lord yes. An hour at least. There in the store. Why?'

'Just a thought. Did Ben seem to mind?'

'Ben? Oh Lord, no. He was talking just as much as

85

Luther. Why, sometimes the two of them would sort of gang up on poor Lola, teasing her and all, until I swear I almost felt sorry for the poor girl at times, but it was obvious she was loving every minute of it. She's a caution, that girl is. Never thought it'd work, when she up and married Ben, and her being half his age and all, but they sure are happy.'

'How far from here to where Ben and Lola live?'

'Ben and Lola? Oh, Lordy, it's probably seven or eight miles. Our road to town and theirs meet up about two miles from the house here. You noticed the fork in the road, didn't you? Did you ride out from town? By the little hogback that's dead ahead coming out from town, when the road forks right to come here to our . . . I mean my ranch; well, the road that forks left there goes right to Ben and Lola's. It's likely closer to seven miles than eight. If you were to go to their place from here, though, you'd cut off three miles anyway by just going as the crow flies. There's one fairly deep gully to cross, going thataway, but it's not a hard ride. I've ridden over to see Lola many a time and it didn't take more'n an hour to get there. Of course, I ride at a good brisk trot. I'm not one of those namby-pamby women who think it's unladylike to straddle a horse and use the stirrups like they're made for.'

'Do you and Lola visit often?'

'No. No not really. Oh, we neighbor a bit, from time to time, but Ben likes for her to stay pretty close to home. She's always sorta different when Ben ain't with her, too. She's such a bubbly thing when Ben's there, but when he's not, she seems kind of, oh, I don't know . . . reserved, like, I guess. Especially with other men. Land sakes, she flirts like a trollop when Ben's there, but not when he isn't. Anyway, Lord knows I've got my hands full here. Especially now, with Luther gone and all, and me wondering if I'm going to have to put on another hand to keep up with things, and where am I going to get the money to do that with?'

'Did Luther neighbor with Ben?'

'Oh, land sakes yes. Why Luther would be over there helping out any time Ben needed help. And, of course, Ben would do the same. We're about the closest neighbors either one has, after all. Land sakes we couldn't make it in this country without folks neighboring back and forth.'

'Any of the Box-3 neighbor back and forth?'

She frowned, trying to make sense of the question.

'The Box-3 is one of the big spreads. Oh, the hands are friendly and all. We don't really have any squabbles over grass and water and things, like they do some places. But no, not really. Three or four of the men will rep for the small guys when the Box-3 does round-up, of course. Oh, once in a while some of the ranch hands from any of the places will stop by for a meal, if they're working cattle close to the place here.'

'They do that at Ben and Lola's too, I suppose.'

'Oh, my land yes! More than here, that's for sure. Every young cowboy in the country finds an excuse to be looking for a lost calf that maybe just happened to wander over there by their place. Land sakes I swear Ben and Lola use twice as much beef as anyone else without them even having a family. Lola, she always cooks for two or three extra people of a noon. She says: 'Somebody might drop by, and I sure wouldn't want them to go hungry.' And, sure enough, some lonely cowboy usually drops by.'

'Does Ben seem to mind that?'

'Land, why would Ben mind that? That man likes to talk as much as any man I ever met.'

'I just wondered if he thought maybe they were stopping by to visit with Lola instead of him.'

'Why, Land o' Goshen! O' course they are. Why, every cowboy in the country's head over heels in love with Lola. But no, it don't bother Ben none. He jokes about it once in a while, but he knows his wife. Lola's half his age, but land sakes there's never been a wife more devoted to her husband than that little lady is. No, Ben he don't worry none about that, leastwise not so far as I've ever been able to tell. A woman can sense things like that, you know. No, I don't think Ben has a jealous bone in his body.'

Eventually, feeling as though he was prying himself from thick molasses, Levi managed to extricate himself from the endless conversation that flowed non-stop from the obviously lonely woman. He rode away frowning in concentration.

He was still turning the conversation over in his mind when an angry buzz whined past his ear. Cursing his carelessness, he dived from the saddle. The flat crack of a rifle which followed hard on the heels of the bullet that narrowly missed him sounded again as he hit the dirt. He tucked his shoulder and rolled as he landed, scurrying on hands and feet behind a tall clump of sagebrush.

The rifle cracked twice more as bullets probed the brush, seeking a chance to encounter something more solid than twigs and leaves.

Moving swiftly, Levi crawled sideways, finding a place from where he could peer through the lower branches. He studied the land in front of him in silence for several minutes of strained silence. The rifle spoke again, three times, closely spaced. Leaves and twigs flew from the brush close to where Levi had left his horse, but none came near him.

He smiled tightly as he spotted tiny wisps of smoke from an outcropping of large boulders just over a hundred yards straight in front of him. He crawled backward slowly, silently. Keeping the tall brush between himself and his attacker, he moved backward until he found a swell of ground that would afford him more substantial cover. Utilizing it to the utmost, he followed it at an oblique angle from the tangle of rocks. As he crawled, the depression he was in deepened until it became a shallow gully.

As soon as he was sure he could do so unseen, he rose to a crouch and ran until he was well beyond the rocks. Then he worked his way at right angles, moving to a position that would place his assailant exactly between himself and where he had started out.

When he was sure he was well positioned, he stood and began to walk, slowly and silently, toward the maze of boulders. They formed the point of a low cliff that emerged for less than a quarter of a mile. He moved stealthily forward until he was against the base of the cliff. Staying tightly against it, he moved around its point. The jumble of large rocks lay slightly below and directly in front of him. He studied them for several minutes, watching for any trace of movement, any hint of sound. There was neither.

Slowly, carefully, he moved forward, sliding like a shadow from rock to rock. Sun glinting off the brass of expended cartridges revealed the location that had been occupied by the shooter. From where he had crouched, the path of Levi's approach lay in a clear field of fire. There was nobody there.

'Must've been nervous,' Levi muttered. 'Couldn't have missed me from here if he wasn't. He sure lit a shuck outa here in a hurry, too.'

Still watching warily, he holstered his gun and walked out into the road. A hundred yards ahead of him his horse still stood in the road, rubbing the side of the bit in his mouth against a front leg, stamping at flies, swishing his tail.

'Guess I'll mount up and see if I can pick up his tracks,' he muttered.

Taking a last look around the rocks he strode the distance to his horse. He picked up the reins and lifted his foot to the stirrup.

'Far enough, Hill,' a voice barked behind him.

The horse shied away from him at the sound of the unexpected voice. Levi whirled. He looked into the barrel of a .44.40 rifle, held at the waist of a stocky, bearded, obviously nervous man. The man's beard was tangled and unkempt. Long, matted hair spilled out from under a ragged hat on to his shoulders. His shirt showed unmistakable signs of wear through the grime that covered it. His voice was tired.

'Figgered you'd be findin' me, sooner er later.'

'Who are you?'

The man shook his head. He took a deep breath and let it out slowly.

'Naw, that ain't gonna work. You know good'n well who I am. I wasn't born just yestiday. I don't know nobody else right around Cheerful that's wanted, so I knowed when I heard you was here that I had to be the reason.'

Levi's eyes darted from the barrel of the rifle to the man's face. There was nothing cold in the expression that faced him, but it was resolute, unflinching. He silently cursed himself for walking into a helpless and hopeless situation as he stalled for time.

'Now I sure hate to disappoint a fella that thinks he knows something, but I didn't come here lookin' for anyone in particular. I don't have any idea who you are.'

The man frowned and shook his head. The almost haunted look in his eyes didn't waver.

'Naw. That there don't make no sense at all. You really don't know who I am?'

Grasping at the hope of engaging the threat to his life in conversation, Levi fought to keep his voice friendly, natural, unhurried.

'I honestly don't have the faintest idea.'

The man took another deep breath. A flicker of doubt crossed his eyes before they went flat again.

'Ever hear o' Ford Whitson?'

Levi frowned thoughtfully. As if deep in thought he moved so that his hand was closer to the butt of

91

the .45 on his hip. Even as he did, a voice in the back of his mind spelled out the reality of his situation. He knew he could normally draw and shoot before the man could squeeze the trigger. He also knew that however much Myra had worked with his hands, they were still stiff from his fight with Ike. His draw would be slower than normal. Not only that, with the grip on the rifle the man held, finger tight against the trigger, his reflexes would squeeze off at least one shot even after he was shot. All that it would accomplish would be that both men would die. Trying to keep the conversation going, he said: 'No, I can't say that I have.'

The man's scowl deepened. 'You wasn't sent up here to find me?'

Levi shook his head. His eyes cast about desperately for something, anything that would serve as a moment's distraction. There was simply nothing that presented itself. He fought to keep his voice casual.

'Sure wasn't. I was sent here to find out who killed the kid that worked in the mercantile store in Cheerful.'

Never allowing the barrel of his rifle to waver from Levi's middle, the man mulled the new idea over for what seemed an interminable amount of time. Eventually he sighed heavily.

'Well, don't that beat all. I could've just kept my mouth shut. Then I went an' missed my chance to bushwhack you. Can't believe I missed ya from that range. But I figgered out what you'd do real good. I knowed sure's anything you'd circle around an' come into them rocks from t'other side, just like you done. So I waited a while after them last shots, then I just plumb walked right over here, quiet like, keepin' to the other side o' this brush so your horse an' your dog wouldn't notice, an' waited for ya to come back. Now I gotta go ahead an' kill ya, though, since I went an' run my mouth off.'

His heart pounding the message that his time was almost run out, Levi fought for seconds, minutes, to try to figure a way out of his hopelessness.

'What are you wanted for?'

'What difference it make?'

'Sorta like to know what I'm gettin' killed for.'

'You're gettin' killed 'cause I went an' got scared, that's all. I just figgered ya was here huntin' me.'

'I'd still sorta like to know what you're runnin' from.'

The man sighed heavily again. The unfathomable sadness in his eyes deepened.

'I went an' shot my ol' lady.'

'Your wife?'

'Yeah. Her an' that two-faced polecat I caught 'er in bed with.'

A sense of outrage and sympathy mingled with Levi's desperation to save his own life.

'Is that so? I'm sorry. That's gotta be hard to handle. But listen for a minute. I doubt if any jury'd ever convict you of murder for that. You might have to serve a couple years in jail, but that'd be better'n runnin' for the rest of your life.'

'Naw, it ain't like that. That fella, he was the kid o' the biggest rancher in the country. I wouldn't stand a chance. I'd be strung up afore I even got to jail.

93

Naw, I can't go back. I'm plumb sorry I gotta kill you, though, seein' as how ya wasn't even after me to start with.'

'Yeah, I'm kinda sorry about that too,' Levi said. Then, as a desperate idea took root in his mind, in a little louder voice he said: 'Blue!'

At the unexpected sound of his name, Levi's horse snorted and tossed his head. Ford's eyes flicked over to the horse for the barest instant. It was the opportunity Levi needed. Normally, it would have been enough. But his hands were so stiff!

He sidestepped quickly. His gun was in his hand, even as he started to move, but it was moving too slowly. Much too slowly. By the time he was half a step to the side, he knew he could never shoot Ford before lead from the rifle riddled his body.

Levi's gun wasn't half-way out of his holster when a round hole mysteriously appeared in the front of Ford's shirt. A fiery ball of lead shattered the hunted man's heart even as his finger tightened on the rifle trigger. The weapon responded with a roar, poking a futile hole in the air where Levi had stood the instant before. Only then did Levi's gun bark, and a second hole appeared in the dying man's shirt.

His eyes bore into Levi as he collapsed forward on to his knees. There was no anger in them, no shock, no pain. Only a deep sadness that seemed to swallow the last spark of a grieving life. His deep sorrow disappeared into emptiness. He pitched forward on to his face and lay unmoving.

Somehow, in the middle of it all, some part of Levi's mind had noted the report of a rifle behind him and to his left. He whirled that way, gun leveled.

Captain Renfro stepped into view, seventy yards away, emerging from behind a tree. He waved at Levi.

'Good move, havin' your horse distract 'im a bit. I was wonderin' how I could plug 'im without 'im goin' ahead an' shootin' ya anyhow.'

Levi tried to answer, but a huge lump in his throat prevented any sound from emerging. He turned back and watched the motionless body of his assailant for several seconds, then slowly replaced the spent round in his .45. A sense of relief flooded through him. He struggled to speak.

'Much obliged, Cap'n. You just happen to be out ridin'?'

Renfro chuckled softly as he walked up beside Levi.

'Heard the shots, earlier. Rode over to check it out. Seen ya comin' back, an' was jist fixin' to holler at ya when this guy steps outa the brush with the drop on ya. I jist shinnied over there behind the tree an' pulled a bead on 'im, waitin' for a chance.'

'I sure owe you one,' Levi acknowledged. 'He'd have killed me, sure's anything. I got in a scrap in town. My hands are still stiff. My draw was plumb slow.'

'Who ya scrappin' with?'

'Ike Canfield.'

The old ranger's eyebrows lifted.

'Now I figgered you fer a smarter man than that. How bad he whip ya?'

'I whipped him.'

Renfro's eyebrows shot upward. 'You whipped Ike Canfield?'

'Yeah. Twice, actually. First time doesn't count, though. I let him have a good right to the chin in the Dusty Soul and put him down once. After he got his head to stop spinnin' he came after me to try again.'

'An' ya put 'im down agin?'

'Yeah, but it took a lot more doin'.'

Renfro chuckled. 'Wal, I'd heard ya was salty. I didn't figger ya'd stand up to Ike, toe ta toe. So who's this here fella?'

Almost instantly a heavy melancholy swept over Levi, as if the dead man's sorrow had taken root in him instead. It was followed by anger at a callow youth and a faithless woman he had never met. He shook his head, unable to form words to express the mixture of emotions that surged through him. He told Renfro the story.

'So he went an' got hisself kilt, jist 'cause of a guilty conscience,' the oldster mused. 'Wal, he ain't the first one. Pity, though.'

'Life sure don't make sense sometimes,' Levi said at last. It was all he could think of to say.

'I 'spect ya'll be haulin' 'im in ta our paragon o' law enforcement,' Renfro offered.

'Yeah, I 'spect.'

'I'd sorta 'preciate it, if'n ya was ta kinda fergit ta mention me.'

'Why's that?'

'Less folks talkin' the better. Word starts spreadin' that I done the shootin', someone might start askin' questions. I'd as soon stay outa the limelight.'

'S'pose Krumm'll notice one hole's from a rifle an' one's from a pistol?'

Renfro gave a short hard laugh. 'Krumm? He won't likely know what kilt the poor feller if'n ya don't tell 'im.'

Levi smiled tightly. 'Prob'ly right. All right. I'll just say I managed to shoot him when he looked away for a second.'

'Much obliged.'

'By the way, you ain't got any good ideas on these killin's, by any chance?'

The old ranger studied Levi for a long moment before he answered.

'I sorta make it a practice not to horn in on another man's investigations.'

Levi nodded. 'Good practice, most times. I gotta tell ya, though, this thing really has me stumped. It seems like the only thing the ones that were killed have in common is that they didn't have an enemy in the world.'

Renfro's nod mirrored his own. He pursed his lips and studied the horizon for a long moment before he spoke.

'They's one other thing in common. Or might be in common. I ain't been able to find out about all of 'em. But I have been nosin' around a mite. Too much ranger in my blood not to ask questions once in a while.'

'And. . . ?'

'Well, the one thing that's started to stick out some is Lola Jordan.'

'Lola? You mean she was foolin' around with the guys that were killed?'

'Nope. Not a bit. Not as fur's I kin tell, anyhow. No,

it ain't thet. But jist a bit afore they up an' got kilt, ever' one of 'em had talked with her.'

'Privately?'

'No, no. I don't 'spect Lola'd likely put herself in thet kind o' position, where folks'd wonder. No, they was all real public conversations. At the mercantile store, in the eatin' place, on the street.'

'Everyone talks to folks around town like that.'

'Thet's a fact. The only thing thet made it sorta stick in my mind was thet everyone what mentioned it remembered thet feller banterin' some with Lola.'

'Flirting?'

'Wal, I 'spect ya could call it thet. Jist funnin' sort o' talk, like fellas always do with a good-lookin' woman. Nothin' outa line, ya understand.'

'Anything Ben was upset about?'

'Thet's the funny thing. Ben, he don't seem to mind atall. Not on the outside, anyhow. He jist goes along with it, acts like he enjoys the attention 'is wife gets, chimes in sometimes an' teases 'er right along with the other fella.'

'You think that's just an act?'

'Now I ain't never figgered a way to tell thet thar. Might not be. He might be jist exactly what 'e seems. On t'other hand, he might jist be a-steamin' inside the whole time.'

'So he waits for his chance and gets rid of the guy he sees as a threat to his marriage.'

'Jist a thought.'

'No evidence to support the idea, I don't suppose.'

'Not a shred. Thet's why I hadn't mentioned it. Jist thought it might be worth yer payin' a bit o' special

98

notice to. Might be a false trail completely.'

'Well, it wouldn't be the first o' those I've ridden. Thanks. I'll work on that angle. Thanks again for savin' my neck today.'

'Keep yer powder dry.'

'Careful! You're giving your age away. Sealed cartridges now, remember?'

The ranger just chuckled quietly as Levi rode away, leading the horse bearing the dead man.

CHAPTER 10

'Well, ya had ta go'n kill a perfectly good man, jist 'cause ya could, huh?'

Levi swallowed the bile that surged into his throat. He kept his voice calm, in spite of the turbulence of his dislike for the town marshal.

'As a matter of fact, I killed a man because he would have killed me if I hadn't.'

'Now that is a real shame,' the marshal retorted. 'Truth be known, I'd ruther have him hangin' 'round Cheerful than you any day.'

'I suppose you knew he was a wanted man?'

' 'Course I knowed he was wanted. I knowed what fer, too. Fer's I'm concerned, he done the right thing. Shouldn'ta had no price on his head ta begin with. He sure wasn't hurtin' nothin' here, an' nobody was no problem fer him, till you had ta come along.'

'Well, then, maybe I'd oughta ask you if you know who's been doing the killings I've been sent to investigate too. Are you hidin' information on that?'

The marshal glared at him.

'Fer's I know, you only been sent to 'vestigate one

killin'. Thet's Les Farmington. Them others ya bin stickin' yer nose inta ain't none o' your concern. An' I ain't got no idee who kilt Les. 'Course, I ain't sure I'd tell ya if'n I did.'

'Yeah, that'd be hard for you, wouldn't it. Doing the right thing, I mean.'

'I do what I figger's right. Now get thet dead body outa here an' take care of 'is buryin'.'

Levi tossed the reins of the dead man's horse on the ground. He glanced at the body lashed across the saddle.

'Naw, I guess that's your problem.'

'Whatd'ya mean?'

'Why, you're the town marshal. Mr Marshal sir, you have a dead body here, that's going to stink up your town something awful in a day or two. I suggest you might want to do something about it. I have out of town business to take care of. Good day, Marshal Krumm.'

He stepped into the saddle and wheeled his horse, kicking him into a brisk trot out of town. He could feel the marshal's eyes boring into his back, but he denied himself the luxury of any glance over his shoulder.

He was still boiling inside as he came into sight of Ben and Lola Jordan's ranch site.

Two dogs barked briefly when he first came into view. They shut up almost immediately, but he didn't hear anyone command their silence. Usually he could hear someone yell at the dogs at least once before they stilled their alarm. Their abrupt silence wasn't the only oddity.

The squat house sat on an open hilltop, with neither trees nor other buildings around it. The barn and corrals sat nearly a hundred yards to the north of the house, nestled against a stand of timber that reached out from a mountain defile. To the south, a thick stand of aspens covered the gently rolling hills that skirted the south-western edge of the mountain spur. Levi sat his horse and frowned at the unusual layout.

Sure didn't look for any shelter from the wind, he muttered. I wonder why they put the house there, instead of over by the timber.

He received the answer to his mental question almost as soon as he rode into the yard.

'Howdy, Hill,' Ben Jordan hailed, stepping to the low-roofed porch. 'You stopped and sized up the place like you're not used to seeing a house set in the open.'

Levi grinned. 'Don't miss much, do you.'

Ben returned the smile. 'Try not to. Neither does Lola. She's the one convinced me we should build it here, like this. She likes to see who's coming afore they get here.'

'Well, you've got a good field of view,' Levi agreed.

'Good field of fire, too, when the Indians was still around more.'

Levi nodded understandingly.

'Not much for anyone to sneak close to the house behind, that's for sure. I see you built it with good shutters, too.'

Ben glanced at the glass windows, each of which was framed by thick, hinged wooden shutters. Each shutter had a cross-shaped opening in the center, to allow a defender in the house both good vision and ability to swing a rifle barrel over a wide area.

'Used 'em twice,' Ben replied.

'That so? Crow?'

'Crow once. A small bunch o' renegade Sioux once. Only half a dozen in each bunch. As luck would have it, we seen 'em soon enough. Shuttered the house. Good moon at night, both times. They lost a couple braves tryin' to rush the house an' gave up. I hope we're past that in this country now.'

'Most likely are,' Levi agreed. 'Especially with the Shoshoni as friendly to whites as they are, and them runnin' both the Sioux and Crow outa the country. Must've been pretty scary for Lola, though.'

Ben nodded vigorously. 'It was for a fact. After the second time, it was about all I could do to persuade her to stay. She was ready to head back East somewhere. She was only fifteen the first time. Seventeen the second.'

'You married young.'

'She was,' he agreed. 'I wasn't that young. She's pertneart fifteen years younger'n me.'

Several questions brimmed Levi's mind, but he pushed them back. The silence hung heavy for half a minute. Ben started, as if suddenly wakening from some reverie.

'Well, now! If I ain't bein' 'bout the rudest bum on the range! Git down an' come in. Standin' here runnin' my chin, and I hadn't even asked ya in. Be stayin' the night, will ya?'

Levi hesitated. 'Well, if it wouldn't put you out . . .'

'Not a bit! You're plumb welcome!' He turned and called over his shoulder. 'Stick another bean in the pot an' another plate on the table, Lola. We got company fer supper.'

As if on cue, Lola Jordan thrust her pretty face around the door jamb.

'Hi, Levi! Good to see you again. Go put your horse in the barn and get washed up. Supper'll be ready in a little bit.'

'He'll be stayin' over,' Ben offered.

'Oh, good,' she replied instantly. 'Always nice to have company.'

By the time they had finished supper, visited a couple hours, and gone to bed, Levi understood fully why every cowboy in the county was in love with Lola. Besides her uncommon beauty, she bubbled with enthusiasm, contributed intelligently to every conversation, and had a delightful laugh that was as infectious as it was enjoyable to hear. Both she and Ben seemed perfectly relaxed in Levi's company.

Even when Levi had deliberately said things that might be construed as flirtatious toward Lola, neither she nor Ben had seemed to notice. They both took his comments as simple compliments, and seemed pleased.

Charolette Walters was right. Ben doesn't seem to have a jealous bone in his body, Levi muttered to himself before he fell asleep. I wonder if it's real, or if that's just for show.

Ben left immediately after breakfast the next morning, without waiting for Levi to leave first.

'Hope you don't take offense,' he explained. 'I've

got some heifers I got to get out to check on, and it's a hard day's ride to get there and back in one day, especially if there's anything needs tended. I don't like to lie out overnight if I can help it.'

'No offense taken,' Levi said swiftly. 'I'll be riding out just as soon as I get my horse saddled.'

'No need to hurry,' Ben assured him. 'Lola'll likely fix you a bait o' lunch to take along, though, if you want 'er to.'

'Sure,' Lola said at once. 'I've got enough left over from fixing yours to make another good lunch. I'll wrap it in oilskin for you.'

Riding off with a good breakfast under his belt and a lunch in his saddle-bags, Levi fought to keep from squirming inside. *I've never seen a man with a wife that pretty that wasn't more protective of her than that*, he fussed. *Especially given his age and hers. He's either the most trusting man I've ever seen, or the dumbest, or the best actor. I wonder which one it is.*

A tiny glimpse from the corner of his eye whipped his head around. The edge of the timber a hundred yards to his left revealed no movement. Yet he was certain some movement there had caught a corner of his vision. He frowned.

A shallow draw fell away to his right. He reined his horse gently toward it, careful to avoid the appearance of any sudden change of plans. In less than 500 yards the bottom of the draw lowered him enough for the hill on his left to cut off his sight of the timber. It also cut him off from the sight of anyone that might be following him.

He stepped out of the saddle and dropped the

reins. He took his rifle from its scabbard and climbed swiftly up the hill, staying low enough to keep below its crest.

At least he thought he did. He miscalculated. His hat, maybe the top of his head even, evidently became visible from the edge of the timber. His hat left his head, tumbling end over end in the air, landing a dozen feet behind him. In the instant after it left his head the sound of a rifle shot reached his ears.

He flopped on to the slanted ground. He raised his head enough to scan the top of the hill. Crawling swiftly, he clambered to his left, then forward, reaching the top of the hill just behind a loose cluster of wild rose-bushes. Hugging the ground, he parted the bushes carefully with his rifle barrel and studied the tree line.

Nothing moved.

There was no sound.

He waited fully thirty minutes. At last he crawled backward until he was again below the protection of the brow of the hill. Then he trotted to retrieve his hat, returned to his horse and mounted.

'Stay behind,' he said softly to the dog, which trotted beside him. The dog immediately dropped back and followed directly behind the horse.

He pushed his mount up out of the draw, and rode parallel to the hill, staying well below any point of visibility from the trees. The animal constantly tried to go either up or down, rather than walk along the slanting ground, but he adamantly insisted on maintaining their relationship to the hill. After half a dozen attempts, the horse complied with his wishes, but expressed his irritation in a trot that was much choppier than normal.

He rode a full mile before once again dismounting. He crawled to the brow of the hill, more carefully this time, picking a spot in a large area of sagebrush to gain a view of the timber, and of his backtrail. Again, nothing moved.

He studied the area for another thirty minutes, then returned to his horse.

'Hunt the man, Curly,' he commanded.

The dog looked at him expectantly. He waved his hat toward the distant line of trees. The dog left in a dead run. He watched Curly disappear into the trees, then settled back to wait. Half an hour later he spotted the dog, trotting across the open space toward him, as if he had no care in the world.

'Well, nobody there now,' he muttered. He mounted, holding his rifle across the pommel of his saddle, and rode directly to the timber. He trusted his dog. He knew nobody would be hiding in the timber the dog had not seen or heard. Even so, the hair stood up on the back of his neck, and his stomach knotted into a hard rock until he gained the cover of the trees. When he did so without drawing any fire, he breathed a heavy sigh of relief.

Riding slowly and silently through the trees, he made his way all the way back to the spot from which the shot had come. He found the tracks of a ridden horse that had remained just inside the trees, paralleling his course. He found where the tracks left the timber, then abruptly changed. He frowned, follow-

107

ing them. After about 400 yards, the tracks changed again, and turned back into the trees. Then they revealed the spot where the hidden rider had sat his horse for quite a while, keeping it where he could see the crest of the hill behind which Levi had been riding.

Levi pushed his hat to the back of his head. 'He figured out what I was going to do to a T!' he breathed. 'Somehow he knew I'd spotted him, or figured I probably did. As soon as I got out of sight, he came out of the trees, kicked his horse into a gallop, came this far, then went back into the trees and waited. He stayed on his horse, so he'd be taller, and he could see me before I expected him to. When my head showed up, he took his shot. Right good shot, too! Didn't miss the top of my head an inch. I bet he thinks he got me. He never bothered to look. He just turned around and rode back. Well, let's see if we can track him.'

He did, but not very far. Within two miles the tracks turned on to the road and mingled with too many others to sort them out.

Somehow, he had a pretty good idea he'd encounter him again, though. In fact, he was sure of it. The next time, he'd be better prepared. He hoped.

CHAPTER 11

'Harm Danver?'

The sheriff looked him over carefully.

'That's me. And, if the descriptions I've been given are anywhere near accurate, you'd have to be Levi Hill.'

Levi smiled. His estimation of the sheriff rose a notch.

'Didn't know I was all that famous.'

'You've made something of a name for yourself all right. What can I do for you?'

'I've been sent up to Cheerful, looking into the murder of a clerk at the mercantile store.'

'Les Farmington.'

Levi's estimation of the sheriff rose another notch.

'That's the one.'

'Then I presume you've met the new standard of competence that challenges law enforcement officers the breadth and width of this fine nation?'

Around his grin, Levi responded: 'I have met the man.'

'And has he taught you any of those astounding new standards of law enforcement?'

'Well, he's taught me new limits to my patience.'

Eyes twinkling, but his face completely impassive, the sheriff replied:

'Patience is a great virtue for detectives. I'm glad to hear that you have benefited from the encounter.'

'Your concern for my well-being is gratifying.'

'How long have you been at Cheerful?'

'Better part o' three weeks.'

'And you haven't busted Krumm's head yet? Or is that what you came to report?'

'Well, truth is I hadn't considered bustin' his head. I didn't figure there was anything in it anyway. I've considered using buckshot on the other end, though.'

The sheriff lost the battle to keep a straight face. Laughing, he rose and extended a hand to Levi.

'It's good to meet you, Levi. I have heard a great deal about you. All good, by the way.'

'Well, you don't want to believe everything you hear.'

'I'll try to keep that in mind. Hero worship is not befitting a peace officer, after all.'

'You got any ideas?'

The sheriff studied him for a long minute.

'Get right down to it, don't you. Mind if I answer your question with a question?'

'Why not?'

'See? You do it too. Do you think the other deaths around Cheerful are connected?'

It was Levi's turn to consider his answer carefully for a full minute. He took a deep breath.

'They gotta be. Too much similarity. Too small an area. There's got to be a common theme and a single killer.'

'Even though they were all killed differently?'

'And had nothing in common.'

'Except meeting a sudden and violent death, for no known reason, with no known enemies.'

Levi nodded. 'You've summed it up pretty well. I take it you've been looking into it.'

'I've ridden around the area. Asked a question or two. Talked with an old friend of mine who ranches over there.'

'Cap Renfro?'

The sheriff's eyebrows rose. 'You've met him.'

'I talked with him a couple times. He saved my bacon a few days ago.'

'That so?'

'Fella had the drop on me. Wasn't connected to the killings, but he was wanted. Figured I was there looking for him. Cap plugged him when he was about to put a hole or two in me.'

'Cap's a good man to have on your side.'

'So do you have any theories you'd be willing to share with Pinkerton?'

'I wouldn't share the time of day with Pinkerton, to be real honest. Ninety per cent of the people Pinkerton has working for him are outlaws and killers, just looking for a chance to strut power they shouldn't have. You, on the other hand, I'd be happy to share information with. Just understand it's in spite of your working for Pinkerton, not because of it.'

Levi's face was troubled as he responded.

'I know a lot of people are down on Pinkerton. I can't deny some of his detectives aren't people I'd turn my back on. But he gets the job done.'

'A lot of innocent people get hurt in the process, too. Anyway, like I said, I'd be happy to share any information I have with you. I've heard a lot about you, and I know you're a straight shooter. Trouble is, I don't have a single shred of information to offer. I'm as stumped over this thing as anything I've run into in more than twenty years of law enforcement.

Levi nodded. 'What do you know about Ben Jordan?'

The sheriff leaned back and studied the ceiling for as much as three or four minutes. His eyes returned to Levi.

'Rancher up above Cheerful. Young wife. Pretty as a picture. Good-natured fellow. Open face. Seems honest. We found four stolen horses on his place four or five years ago. He had a bill of sale for all four. Some riders passing through needed fresh mounts, so they traded horses with him. Gave him the bills of sale. No reason to think he knew they were stolen. He offered them up right away when he found out they were. No argument at all.'

'Know who the riders were?'

'Yeah. We found 'em. Still had the money they'd stolen on 'em. Took the horses they were riding back to Jordan after we hung 'em. We figured he'd ought to at least get his own horses back. Why are you interested in him?'

'Cap's hunch, more'n mine. He thinks the guys that got killed might've been flirting with Jordan's wife, so he slipped around and killed 'em.'

The sheriff considered it briefly. 'Well, that's sure possible. Guys that marry a woman that much younger get pretty jealous sometimes. Especially when she's that pretty. Doesn't square with my impression of the man, though. He didn't act the least bit sneaky or back-handed.'

'Yeah, that's my problem with it, too.'

'Who was the guy Cap shot?'

'Fella name of Ford Whitson.'

Harm reflected several heartbeats before answering.

'Wanted for killing his wife and her lover. That the guy?'

'That's him.'

'Well, not likely he had any connection to the killings. He'd have been lying low, most likely.'

'You know anybody else around the area that might be the sort to kill folks for no apparent reason?'

'Nope. I'm as buffaloed over it as I can be. There's been what, now – four?'

'Five, if you count Funderburke.'

'Who's Funderburke?'

'Homesteader. Froze to death last winter. His wife – widow, that is – is sure he was killed. She said he had a big knot above one ear. She thinks someone cracked his skull and left him to freeze to

113

death in the storm.'

'Is that so? I hadn't even heard about that. I might've heard about him freezing, but wouldn't have paid any attention, if it didn't look like a crime. So, there's been five.'

'Looks that way.'

'Well, I'd be glad to ride down that way with you, do what I can. Can't think what I could do to help, though. Other than get Krumm all riled up, that is. He acts as though a wolverine dug into his hen-house every time I show up.'

'Well, that'd give him someone besides me to be put out with. I guess you're right, though. If I need some reinforcements, I'll sure holler, though.'

'You do that. Of course, from what I've heard, if you need reinforcements, you probably need the army.'

He nodded to Levi's horse, standing at the hitch rail. The ragged yellow dog sat beside the horse's front leg, panting patiently. The sheriff's eyes took in the two scabbards attached to the saddle instead of the one most cowhands had. The .30.30 rifle was in the one below his left leg, stock forward. On the other side of the saddle, stock toward the rear, a fatter scabbard held the twelve-gauge Colt revolving shotgun.

His eyes swung back to Levi himself. His usual .45 was low on the hip, tied down. A second gun, butt forward, rode his left side at belt-level. Just behind the left gun, a large knife fit snugly in its sheath.

'I notice you ride pretty well-heeled. From what

I've heard, you didn't use to pack the second pistol.'

Levi smiled. 'I got a thing about being out-gunned.'

'Well, about all you're missin' is a gatlin' gun. You could maybe put one o' them on a pack-mule.'

With a perfectly straight face Levi responded:

'I've thought some about it. Either that or a six-pounder like the cavalry haul around.'

'It'd be pretty hard to draw in a hurry, I'd think.'

Levi flexed his arms with a mock seriousness.

'I been buildin' up my shoulders. I figure as soon as I get to where I can pick it up and hold it while it shoots, I'll maybe take one along.'

'Now that'd be a sight to see.' The sheriff chuckled. 'If you ain't careful that'll get written into some song and you'll be as famous as Pecos Bill.'

Abruptly Levi grew tired of the banter.

'If you hear anything, I'd sure appreciate a holler.'

'I'll get word to you if I do. Count on it.'

Levi rode out of town convinced there was at least one honest lawman in the county.

All the way back to Cheerful he turned the facts over and over in his mind. Nothing new occurred to him. Nothing made sense. He was less than five miles from Cheerful when he looked over his shoulder at the sound of approaching hoof-beats. His hand dropped to the butt of his .45.

A lone rider raised a hand to him as he approached at a fast trot.

'Howdy, Hill! Mind if I ride along? Gettin' kinda tired o' ridin' alone.'

Levi kept his face impassive. It was the first time he

had seen the young cowboy since their encounter in Shedd's store.

'Denton, ain't it?'

The cowboy grinned. 'That's me. Bucky Denton. We talked a couple times in town.'

'Yeah, I thought I remembered you.'

'You makin' any headway?'

'What's that?'

'You makin' any headway? You know. You gettin' any closer to figgerin' out who went an' killed all them fellas?'

Levi fought to keep the irritation out of his voice.

'Why do you ask?'

'Jist wonderin'. Jist like everyone else around, I reckon. Bad thing. Gotta figger out who's doin' it an' get rid of 'im. Can't have someone around that kills everyone he gets mad at.'

'Yeah, it's a bad business,' Levi agreed. 'Not much information to go on, though.'

'Well, I don't know. I ain't a lawman or nothin', but it don't seem that mysterious to me. Kinda obvious, actually.'

Hoping the bile in his throat didn't affect his expression, Levi said:

'Really? You got it figured out, do you?'

'Sure. Well, I ain't plumb sure, but I think so. Seems plumb obvious.'

'Well, maybe you could share it with me, since I don't seem able to see it.'

'Ben Jordan.'

'What?'

'Gotta be Ben Jordan.'

'Why do you say that?'

The young cowboy's face had lost its open smile. His eyes glinted with an intensity that tensed his whole body. His words sounded as if the end of each was bitten off as it left his mouth.

'Ben went an' married Miss Lola when he knew good and well he was way too old for her. A man that age can't possible keep a woman like Miss Lola happy. He knows it good and well. He's so jealous of her that he just boils inside every time she talks to someone close to her own age. It don't show on his face, but I can see it. It just plumb eats him up.'

'You think he's the one who's doing the killing?'

Denton nodded vigorously.

'Listen. I hang around town quite a lot. I got to thinkin' about it. Every one of those guys who was killed was comin' on to Miss Lola somethin' awful, just a day or two afore they got killed. Every one of 'em.'

'Well, I don't know about that.'

Denton's intensity increased. 'I'm tellin' you, that's the connection. You saw it, once, yourself. There in the mercantile store. That two-bit green-horn gambler was shinin' up to Miss Lola like she was one o' them whores at the Dusty Soul. Smilin' an' laughin' like he had any business even talkin' to the likes o' Miss Lola! Sayin' stuff like he was sayin'! More'n jist disrespectful. He was jist plumb flirtin' with her, that's what he was doin'. An' Ben was watchin' an' listenin', knowin' good an' well that gambler was jist tryin' to get somethin' started with Miss Lola. But he don't never show it, Ben don't. He

117

jist smiles an' laughs, an' acts like he ain't jealous. But I know good an' well he was jist plumb boilin' inside. Then right after that, what happens? That two-bit gambler turns up deader'n a doornail. Don't take too much to put two an' two together.'

'What about Steiger?'

'The cowboy?'

'Yeah. He hadn't been around town for almost a month.'

'That don't mean he wasn't shinin' up to Miss Lola. Jist the day afore he got kilt, he up an' went right out to their place to see 'er.'

'Steiger was seeing Lola when Ben wasn't around?'

'Oh, Ben, he was there all right enough. Jist like always, actin' like he was jist enjoyin' the conversation an' all, but all the time I know good an' well 'e was boilin' like everything.'

'Well, how did you know Steiger was there? Were you out there?'

'Well, yeah. I rode by, lookin' fer some calves. Invited me in fer dinner, they did. An' that Steiger, he was jist goin' on an' on to Miss Lola. Even I could tell he was plumb smitten with 'er. Stayed there even after Ben an' me both left. Miss Lola, she said she was gonna fix 'im some lunch to take along. Then, next day, he turns up dead jist like the rest.'

'Well, I'll think about it.'

'You better do more'n think about it! I'm tellin' ya, Ben, he's gonna keep on killin' folks till someone stops 'im. He's one tough man, Ben Jordan is, but I'm bettin' you kin take him. You better get to doin' it, too. I know good an' well he's gonna kill someone else if you don't.'

With that the cowboy clamped the spurs to his horse and rode off in a cloud of dust. Levi's frown followed him thoughtfully.

CHAPTER 12

If he followed the laughing young river around one more point of land, he would be able to hear the falls. He knew the land well enough to know the copse of aspen bunched against a tall cliff provided the best campsite for miles.

Levi had spent the whole day trying to backtrack the young cowboy who had accosted him as he approached Cheerful three days before. Something about the man bothered him. He just couldn't put a finger on what it was.

Tomorrow he'd ride over to Ben and Lola Jordan's ranch. Several approaches scratched around in his mind for feeling Ben out a little better. Men had killed out of jealousy of a young wife before. If Ben were feeling his age, afraid his wife was less than satisfied, it would fit the pattern.

The ears of Levi's horse shot forward. At almost the same instant Levi caught the glimpse of a horse's tail as it switched back and forth, its tip barely visible from behind a clump of trees.

Looking about swiftly, he reined his own horse around a screening patch of wild plum bushes and dismounted swiftly. Just as swiftly his rifle slid out of its scabbard and his boots landed lightly on the ground.

'Stay here, Curly,' he whispered to his dog. The dog obediently sat down beside the horse.

He worked his way through the brush, moving silently, until he could see across the clearing. From his vantage point he could see the rump of a horse, but nothing else that moved. The horse idly swished at flies with its tail. One rear hoof was cocked up on the tip of the hoof, as the horse rested his leg. Then he spotted a second one.

'Been standin' a while,' he muttered silently to himself. 'Wonder who's there an' why?'

He moved stealthily back to his horse. Working quickly, he replaced his boots with a pair of moccasins from a saddle-bag. He hung his hat on the saddle horn. Then he looked around again, and chewed his lower lip thoughtfully.

He picked up the trailing reins of the horse. 'C'mon, Blue,' he whispered. 'Quiet, Curly.'

Leading the horse, with the rangy dog trotting obediently behind, he led the animals a hundred yards away, into a shallow, brush-choked gully that angled toward the end of the red cliff. He tied the horse's reins to the brush, keeping the animal where he wouldn't be seen by anyone chancing to ride by.

'Stay with 'im, Curly,' he said softly.

Instantly the dog laid down near the horse. Moving as silently as a shadow Levi moved out in a long circle that brought him to the base of the cliff nearly 300 yards from the horses he had seen. Taking advantage of every bit of cover he moved without sound along the cliff and into the trees.

As he entered the shade of the grove of aspen, it felt as if the temperature dropped twenty degrees. Levi wiped the sweat from his brow with a shirt-sleeve, allowing his eyes time to adjust fully to the lesser light of the dense growth.

A low murmur of voices reached him, too distant to make out any words. He looked around, double-checking to be sure he was on the opposite side of the people to the horses he had seen. There was no danger of stumbling on to the horses and betraying his presence through them. He stole soundlessly toward the soft voices, keeping in a crouch, placing each foot carefully to avoid any twigs or anything that would cause a sound.

As he neared, he realized the voices were those of a man and a woman. The man's voice was followed by a woman's giggle. He frowned, considering reversing his course.

'Sounds like I found somebody's hideaway,' he muttered.

A dozen scenarios ran through his mind before he decided he needed to know who it was. 'At least the voice ain't Myra's,' he reassured himself.

Lips compressed tightly, Levi maintained his course until the sounds told him the couple was just beyond the brush that lay directly before him. He slid down on to his belly and moved forward with infinite patience, making no sound whatever.

With his rifle barrel he moved a branch enough to

give him a clear view of a flat clearing, covered with lush grass. Almost to the far edge of the clearing, a man was just pulling up his pants. He fastened his belt, then sat down on the grass to pull on his boots. As he did, his face turned toward Levi. He struggled to keep from gasping aloud. It was Ben Jordan.

His eyes darted to the woman, who was seated on a blanket, just finishing the job of putting her own clothes back on. From the description Myra had given him, Levi was sure the woman was Maria McCallum.

She had talked about Maria and her husband, Sean, when Levi had brought up the subject of Ben and Lola's age difference. Sean was barely twenty, but Maria was well into her thirties at least. The age difference, in the opposite direction from Ben and Lola, was more curious to Levi than the Jordans'. He thought it was just somehow odd that a young cowboy would be so infatuated with a woman that much older than himself.

As he watched, Maria stood up, straightening her clothes. Ben tossed a ten-dollar gold piece to her. She snatched it out of the air and it disappeared into her clothing someplace so quickly Levi didn't know where she had put it.

'I never know making money is so much fun before I meet you,' she laughed at Ben.

'Woman, you are worth every cent an' then some!' Ben shot back at her. 'You gotta be the finest hunk o' woman any man ever had a tumble with. I spent ten years tryin' ta teach Lola how ta do some o' them things, and she either can't learn er won't. What I wonder, though, is how you explain the extra money to that young pup you're married to.'

Maria laughed lightly. 'He is more of the man than you might think. Anyway, he is so silly, it is no problem,' she replied. 'He is so much in love with Maria he cannot think of anything else. I tell him I sell the lace that I tat at the store in town. It is the only way I can have the nice clothes I like to wear. My husband, he just say how lucky he is to have a wife that make love like me and make money too. Besides, if he get mad at me, all I need to do is wiggle my hips at him and he forget what he was almost to get mad about.'

'He can't have any idea what he's got,' Ben observed.

Maria snorted, tossing her long black hair.

'Maybe. Maybe he does not. Maybe because he is so soon done he don't have no time to find out neither. He is so foolish a young boy, but he is good to Maria. Besides, I know where to find a fine lusty old stallion when I need one who knows what he is doing. I wonder sometimes if even two women are enough to keep you happy.'

Ben chuckled as he strapped his gun on and tied the holster down.

'You sure do know how to make an old stallion feel like a young stud, that's for sure.' He strode to the woman and swept her into his arms, kissing her passionately. 'That'll keep ya thinkin' about me till the next time,' he teased. 'I gotta get ridin' fer home. You'll be here next week?'

'Wild horses could not keep Maria away!'

He strode away in the direction of the horses. She

124

quickly folded up the blanket and followed.

Levi lay in the bush without moving for a long while. He heard both horses leave, Ben's horse trotting swiftly toward the LJ-Bar, and Maria's more slowly in the opposite direction. He heard without noticing the high-pitched buzzing of gnats around his face. He heard the deeper buzz of a deer-fly, the chatter of a jay and the distant squawking of a magpie, with no conscious thought of their presence.

'Well, so much for wonderin' if he's still man enough to keep a younger woman satisfied,' he muttered. 'That just muddies up the water somethin' awful. Would a man who's foolin' around on his wife be jealous enough of her to kill anyone who flirts with her? That doesn't make any sense at all.'

He slid out from under the cover of the brush and walked back to his horse. Curly nuzzled him as he replaced the moccasins with his boots.

'Good boy,' he commended the patient dog. 'Let's ride back to town and see if Myra can make any sense outa this mess.'

He was still frowning with the unwanted information he had learned when he put his horse in the livery barn, fed him and the dog, and headed up the street toward Myra's house. If he hadn't been so deep in thought he would have seen them before they were so close.

When it registered that three men were standing in the street waiting for him, the alarms in his mind finally shoved the confusion from his consciousness. Instinctively he undid the snap that held the strap over the butt of his .45 and tucked the strap behind the holster, out of the way. His hand stayed there, just brushing the polished walnut of the grip.

Twenty-five feet in front of him Ike Canfield, flanked by two other men, walked slowly toward him. The one on Canfield's right Levi pegged as Frosty Summers. He had never met the man, but descriptions of an outlaw who cropped up frequently around Kaycee fit him to a T. The one on the other side of Canfield was smaller. His nose and ears appeared too large for his otherwise fine-featured face. The effect was to give him a hawkish look. His eyes filled out that image, staring at Levi with the cold absence of emotion common to predators. Low on his right hip a pearl-handled Colt jutted from a smoothly oiled holster. The pearl grips were worn smooth from countless encounters with the gunman's hand. It was he whom Levi instantly identified as the most dangerous of the three.

'Evenin', Ike,' Levi offered.

'You ruint me, Hill,' Canfield responded.

'I ruined you? How do you figure that?'

'I ain't never been whipped afore. You went an' done it twice. The first time I could say I didn't see it a-comin'. Then you went an' whipped me again. Thet ruint me.'

'We've all been whipped a few times, Ike. There's no shame in that. You fought a good fight.'

'Don't matter none. You whipped me. You ruint me.'

'Now why should it be that bad to get whipped? Like I said, it happens to all of us.'

'Not to me. Thet's how I made my way. The boys, they allays done what I said, 'cuz they knowed nobody in the world could whip me. Er outshoot me neither, fer thet matter, but mostly whip me. My whole life there hadn't never been no man alive what could do that. Now they is, but they can't be.'

'What do you mean?'

'I mean it's still gotta be true that they ain't no man alive what ever whipped me.'

'I whipped you. Twice. The last time I checked, I was still breathin' just fine.'

'Yeah, well thet there's what's gonna change. We come ta kill ya, Hill.'

'Think about that, Ike. Is it worth a hangin', just to say you've never been whipped by any man alive?'

Ike blinked at him several times before he answered.

'We ain't aimin' ta hang. They ain't no law in Cheerful 'ceptin' Krumm.'

'There's Harm.'

Ike glanced quickly at each of his companions in turn. He swallowed. Then he took a deep breath and squared his shoulders.

'Don't matter none. He ain't likely ta ketch up with us. Don't matter. We come ta kill ya, so go fer yer gun, Hill.'

'Now!' the small man on Ike's right said.

He was reaching for his gun even as he said the word. His hand closed on the worn pearl grips at almost the same instant the first bullet from Levi's .45 slammed into his chest. A look of stunned disbelief crossed his face. He rolled his eyes downward,

127

trying in vain to see what had hit him so hard and unexpectedly.

So swiftly it sounded almost like a continuation of the first shot, Levi's gun barked again. It caught Frosty Summers in the right shoulder just as his gun cleared the top of its holster and leveled on Levi's chest. The gun tumbled from the suddenly numb and senseless fingers, even as the bullet that left its barrel ripped a hole through Levi's vest. Frosty was driven back and turned by the force of the slug that shattered his shoulder.

Levi's gun swivelled back to bear on Ike. The big man's draw was far, far faster than Levi had anticipated. His gun was already in his huge fist, bellowing fire at the man who had humiliated him. Only his haste and seething anger could have caused him to miss at that range. Levi felt the angry heat of the bullet as it whined past his ear. His own bullet hammered the big man in the chest at almost the same instant.

Ike grunted and took a step backward, then brought his gun back into line with Levi, sending forth another missile of death that tugged at Levi's shirt-sleeve. Levi's gun barked a second, then a third time.

Each hot pellet of lead that plowed into his chest drove another grunt from Ike's lips. He took a step backward with one foot to maintain his balance as he fought for strength to lift the gun that had been knocked out of alignment with his adversary by the force of the bullets striking him.

Out of the corner of his eye Levi saw Frosty pulling

a gun from his waistband with his left hand. He swung his .45 that way and squeezed the trigger twice. The gun barked and the first slug took the outlaw squarely in the jaw, driving through his teeth and out the back of his head. He was dead before the hammer on Levi's gun fell with a hollow click on an empty chamber.

Levi stepped quickly to his right as he holstered his gun. The hand that dropped the gun in its sheath never slowed. It continued in the same smooth motion to draw the gun that rode, butt forward, on his left hip. As it cleared the holster Levi turned his left side away from the hand, expediting the draw and turning sideways to Ike, offering a narrower target. That gun came up and into line with Canfield's chest at the same instant Ike's gun barked again, sending a slug into the space Levi had vacated by the sidestep and turn.

Levi fired three times in rapid succession, sending three more blows of hot death into the big man's chest. Even as the third one struck, Ike's knees buckled. His eyes glazed over. He crumpled into the street like a rag-doll.

Myra ran into the street, holding her dress high enough to keep from tripping in it.

'Levi! Levi! Are you all right?'

Levi stood with his gun hanging at arm's length, suddenly too weak to answer. All he could think of was an overwhelming desire to get away from there, to bury his face in Myra's hair, hold her to himself, and find something in Cheerful to be cheerful about.

129

CHAPTER 13

He surprised himself by sleeping soundly. It was against every instinct, he thought. Somehow, some deeper awareness within knew better than his conscious mind when he was safe.

The morning sun threatened the bleak sky with its coming flood of brilliance when he awoke. An instant of panic raced through his mind as he realized how soundly he had slept. It was replaced almost at once by an unaccustomed indolence. The feather bed felt like heaven beneath him. The quiet of the house seemed like a cocoon of serenity and safety. He suddenly longed for a life in which he could awaken like that every day, with a devoted wife asleep beside him. The thought of Myra's form filling the other half of the bed popped unbidden into his mind.

He shook the thought away angrily. That was not the life he had chosen. It would do no good to allow himself to wish for what could no longer be.

Still, Cap Renfro had managed. If a man as famous among the Texas Rangers as he had been could disappear and build a new life like that, why not Levi Hill?

He made a stronger effort to force the thought from his mind. Quiet rustling in the house's other bedroom helped him clear his mind. Silently he slid from the bed and dressed. He eased outside and abruptly remembered the problem with a house that sat in the middle of a large clearing. There were no bushes to step behind to relieve himself. He settled for a spot a few steps away from the corner of the house by the room in which he had slept. At least he knew nobody would inadvertently see him there.

He instinctively checked the sky, the breeze, the temperature, the normal noises of the Wyoming morning, all without even being aware he was doing so. When he re-entered the house, Lola was busily preparing breakfast.

'Sleep well?' Ben greeted him.

'I slept like a log,' Levi responded. 'Can't remember sleeping like that for a long time.'

'I thought lawmen always slept light,' Lola offered.

Levi frowned. 'Normally I do that, for a fact. I hear about every mouse that walks and every owl that swoops down to catch it. I sure didn't last night.'

'You must feel safe at our house.'

'Yeah, as a matter of fact, I do,' Levi admitted. 'Maybe it's knowing how you've got the house situated, and knowing the dogs would wake us up if anything was comin'.'

Ben nodded. 'That helps a bunch, that's for sure. I've been glad a bunch o' times that Lola insisted on it. So what's in your plans for the day?'

'Well, I thought I'd ride up toward Harvey Peak, where Walters was killed. Couple things about the set-up there that still have me baffled. His death doesn't make any more sense than any of the others.'

'No suspects at all yet, huh?'

Levi wasn't at all sure why he said what he said next.

'Well, none except you.'

Lola stopped with a skillet in her hand, suspended just above the stove top, and stared at him. Ben was just lifting a cup of coffee to his lips. It stopped in the same instant, suspended like the skillet. It was as if time suddenly stopped, freezing the scene in mid-action.

After several heartbeats of silence, Ben said: 'Me?'

Levi took a careful sip of the scalding coffee Lola had set before him.

'Yeah, as a matter of fact two or three people have mentioned you.'

'Why in the world would anyone think Ben had anything to do with those murders?' Lola demanded.

'You.'

'Me?'

'You ain't makin' no sense,' Ben protested. 'In the first place, you don't agree with them folks, whoever they are, or you wouldn't be stoppin' off here now an' then. You sure wouldn't be sleepin' that sound if you thought I was a killer.'

'A man sure wouldn't think so,' Levi agreed.

'So who says I got somethin' to do with it?'

'Just people guessin', that are as stumped as I am.'

'Well, why? Why would I go killin' folks?'

'The way it was told to me, the only thing all the fellas that got killed had in common was that they was flirtin' with Lola some, just before they got killed. Some folks think you're jealous enough to get rid of anyone you think pays her too much attention.'

Lola's mouth sagged open. Ben studied Levi's face for a long moment, then broke into a long and hearty laugh. By the time he stopped laughing, Lola was smiling too. She resumed the breakfast preparations.

'Well, the idea that was offered was that you notice the fellas that pay special notice o' Lola, then you follow 'em somewhere and get rid of 'em.'

Ben shook his head in disbelief. 'Man, if I did that, I'd be one busy man. There wouldn't be more'n a dozen or so men left alive in the county. And the ones that were would all be over sixty.'

'Maybe,' Levi argued. 'On the other hand, the idea makes sense. You're quite a bit older'n Lola, and she is a beautiful woman. And, the fact is, I haven't been able to find one single thing besides that to tie all these murders together. It's the only idea anybody's come up with that makes sense.'

'Well, that don't make sense neither,' Ben insisted.

'Why not?'

'Well, it, it just don't. There's reasons. If you knowed the reasons, you'd understand.'

'Then I guess I need to know the reasons.'

Ben shook his head slowly. He lifted his cup of coffee and scowled into it as he sipped. He set it down again.

'Them ain't fer you to know.'

Levi shifted in his chair and frowned into his own coffee. Over the cup's rim he studied Ben and Lola in turn. Ben was staring fixedly at the table. Lola was frozen at the stove, skillet in mid-air, staring at her husband.

After a long, painful silence, Lola spoke. Her voice was so soft Levi almost couldn't hear her words.

'Let me tell him, Ben.'

Ben's head jerked up. He stared at his wife for a long moment. He jerked his head back and forth once in a forceful refusal, and dropped his eyes again.

'Please, Ben,' her soft voice pleaded. 'He has a right to know.'

Ben's eyes lifted to Levi. Levi flinched at the pain mirrored in the rancher's look. Ben's eyes darted to Lola, then back to Levi, then down to the table once again.

'Please?' she pleaded. 'He'll never say anything. I know we can trust him. He has a right to know.'

Ben's eyes slowly lifted to his wife. He studied her face, watching as a single tear trickled from a corner of her left eye.

'You sure?' he said, as softly as her own voice had been.

She nodded, ignoring the tear.

'I'm sure. It's time I told somebody, anyway.'

Ben sighed heavily. He abruptly lifted his cup and drained it of coffee. He set the cup back on to the table with a bang.

'Well, then, tell it if you gotta.'

Lola watched him for several heartbeats before

her eyes shifted to Levi. She took a deep breath.

'Please never tell anyone,' she asked.

Levi's frown deepened.

'Well, before you go telling me something, I'm not sure I can promise that. If it isn't something I have to tell, in the line of duty, then I can promise. If it has to do with a crime of some kind you committed, or something like that, then I couldn't make that promise.'

She nodded. 'I understand that. It isn't anything like that.'

He nodded. 'Then you have my word.'

She stared into the space above his head until the silence began to crowd into the empty spaces of the small kitchen. A second tear followed the path the first had blazed across the beauty of her cheek.

She began to speak. The words gained speed, as if they had to be released quickly or they would not flow, or as if the dam that had held them too long in check had suddenly burst.

'The fact is, Levi, that I enjoy the teasing and the flirting, but I would never, ever, let it lead to anything beyond that. Ben knows that, very well. Too well, maybe. The, the truth is, that I . . . I have never . . . that I don't like that part of marriage . . . very much. The idea that he is too old to satisfy me is . . . absurd. I . . . I'm afraid the shoe is entirely on the other foot.'

'She's got her reasons,' Ben offered.

She lifted a hand to restrain him from trying to help her tell her story.

'Before I met Ben, when I first came to this country, I was with my family. North-east of here a hundred miles or so, we were attacked by Indians.'

'Sioux,' Ben said softly.

She ignored the interruption.

'My father refused to travel with a wagon train. He thought it was safer with a single wagon. We could stay out of sight better. Camp where our fire would-n't be seen. He never thought about the wagon making tracks that the Indians could follow as easily as if he made a map for them. They found us, of course.'

Tears flowed suddenly, as if the dam holding them had also broken. She sat down in a chair and covered her face with her apron. Her shoulders shook, but she made no sound. Ben rose from his chair and moved over to stand beside her. He put an arm around her shoulders and pulled her over against him.

After several minutes she straightened and lowered the apron. Ben relaxed his arm, but kept a reassuring hand on her shoulder.

'There were five of us. My two brothers, my parents and me. My brothers were . . . Lloyd was sixteen. Martin was eleven. I was thirteen. There were only seven Indians in the bunch, but they were hidden. We couldn't ever even see them, until they would stand up to shoot, then they'd disappear again. My mother and my brothers were all really good shots, and they tried to defend us. They just couldn't see the Indians. They were all killed.'

'Except you,' Levi suggested.

'I always wished. . . . I . . . . Yes. All but me.'

'They . . . one of them . . . snuck up behind me

and grabbed my rifle out of my hands. Then he hollered to the rest of them. They all just ... it seemed like they just rose up out of the ground. They were so close! And I hadn't even seen them. Then they started laughing and stringing all of our things out of the wagon all over the ground. They tore all my clothes off, and started taking turns. . . . They . . .'

A shudder ran through her body at the memory, continuing until Levi thought it would become a complete fit, but she asserted control over herself and calmed.

'They used her plumb hard,' Ben said.

She held up her hand to her husband again.

'They did,' she agreed, 'until ... until I heard a gunshot. It was a big boom. It was a bigger gun than I'd ever heard. And the Indian that was getting ready to ... that was about to ... the one closest to me was knocked flat on the ground. The one holding me down let loose and stood up, and the big gun boomed again, and he was knocked flat, like he'd been hit with a big club or something. The other Indians started talking, and they just disappeared. They must have dropped into the grass and brush or something, and started sneaking away. The gun fired again, and I could hear the bullet hit something, so I knew whoever was shooting had spotted one of them and hit him. Then there wasn't anything any more.'

'It was me,' Ben offered. 'Me'n my Sharps fifty. I'd heard the commotion an' was ridin' to figger out what it was. From the top of a ridge I spotted the wagon an' the bodies, an' them savages havin' their fun with the one that wasn't dead. I settled down in the grass an' started pickin' 'em off. I ended up gettin' four outa the seven afore the others got to their horses an' hightailed it.'

Lola took up the story again.

'It seemed like I lay there forever. I was afraid to move. And I hurt so bad I thought I was going to die anyway. I didn't know anything could ever hurt like that.'

'She was just a little thing, Thirteen years old.'

Ignoring him, she continued. 'Then someone tossed a blanket over me. I had my eyes shut, because I was afraid to look. Then I heard the nicest, kindest voice I have ever heard in my life. He said, 'Are you able to talk?''

'I didn't know but what they mighta cut out 'er tongue too,' Ben explained. 'They been known to do that, if a woman won't stop screamin'.'

'He asked me if I was hurt, other than what they were doing to me.'

Ben smiled. 'She opened her eyes and looked at me. I ain't never seen eyes that beautiful afore nor since. She saw I was a white fella, an' she wrapped her arms around me an' hung on like she thought I was gonna run away.'

'I knew I never wanted to let loose of that man,' she agreed. 'And I never have.'

Ben cleared his throat. 'But, the point is ... I mean, what she's tryin' to make ya understand, Levi, is that they'd done used her plumb hard. Kinda ruint 'er fer a woman, you know?'

'What he means is that I have had a very hard time ever being a good wife to Ben. I love him with every

138

fiber of my being. I just can't . . . I don't very often . . .'

'I'm a good bit older'n she is,' Ben said again. 'I nursed 'er back to health. She was with me for a couple years afore I talked her into marryin' me. I convinced her I didn't need a hot-blooded young wife.'

Lola's eyes pleaded desperately with him.

'Do you understand? In all that time, before I agreed to marry him, he never tried to touch me. He never does, even now, even though we're married, unless it's my idea, because I just can't stand to have a man . . .' Her eyes pleaded with him. 'Ben doesn't have to worry, or be jealous, or wonder if I'm going to find some younger man attractive.'

Levi stared into the half-dozen grounds in the bottom of his coffee cup. The picture came into perfect focus in his mind. Her need to have the house with no cover within rifle-shot around it. Ben's lack of any hint of jealousy. Even the scene in the hidden tryst with Maria suddenly made perfect sense. The wrong and the inevitability of that relationship fought valiantly in his mind. At least he had a clear picture of the situation. And the pain.

He just had absolutely no murder suspects.

Not even one. Not any more.

CHAPTER 14

Levi rode away from the Jordans' L-J Bar frowning in thought. On a whim he wheeled his horse and headed straight toward the mountains. Charolette Walters just might be able to shed some light on a picture that had gone from dim and hazy to completely black.

The change of direction brought him through a grove of trees about 400 yards from the L-J Bar ranch house. As he skirted the thickest of the trees he reined his horse abruptly. He slid from the saddle and walked forward, bent over, studying the ground.

Curly followed at his heels, sniffing the ground.

Levi stood and stared around him, carefully noting every tree, every branch, every clump of brush. He returned to his horse. Removing his moccasins from a saddle-bag, he quickly replaced his boots with the soft buckskin.

'Stay behind me, Curly,' he said softly.

As he melted soundlessly into the trees, the coarse-haired dog padded silently behind him. Several times Levi stopped. Following a trail most eyes would never see, he worked his way to the edge of the trees nearest the ranch house. He retraced his steps and followed parallel to the tree-line until he spotted another trail, then followed it to the trees' edge. He continued the pattern several times. Each time he would turn and return deeper into the trees, then follow another nearly invisible trail to a similar vantage point.

An hour later he returned to his horse. He replaced the moccasins in the saddle-bag and put his riding-boots back on. He leaned across the saddle, resting with both forearms on it, lost in thought.

Curly whined softly. Levi turned and dropped to a crouch. The dog laid his nose across his thigh. He scratched the dog's ears and petted him while he thought.

'Well, Curly, it gets nuttier all the time. Somebody's been slippin' into these trees, watching the Jordans' place. Quite a few times. Cowboy. Boots are pretty worn. Leaves his horse way back, so it won't give 'im away. But it's a long way from the house. Four hundred yards at least. Can't see much from that far away.'

He mulled it over in his mind a while longer, then rose. 'Let's ride a circle, Blue. We'll see if it's only from this side.'

He spent the next three hours riding a complete circle around the Jordan ranch. Staying well behind the last stand of timber before the ranch's clearing, he found more than a dozen places where the same person had watched their ranch for extended periods of time.

Abruptly his horse's ears shot forward. Curly growled once. Levi dived from the saddle. A bullet ripped a small branch from a tree just to the left of where he had been an instant before. A rifle shot echoed, bouncing from rocks and cliffs until it was impossible to tell from what direction it had come.

Using the direction his horse's ears had pointed as his only guide, Levi drew his gun and raced as soundlessly forward as his boots would allow. As he broke into a small clearing he heard the swift retreat of running hoofs somewhere ahead of him.

He stopped, listening to the fading sounds. His lips pressed tightly together. He shook his head once. 'That's about three times that fella's just barely missed me,' he gritted. 'I gotta get my head workin' before he tries again. He ain't likely to keep missin'.'

He holstered his gun and walked back to his horse. He followed the tracks of his attacker until they merged into the main road. Again.

As the sun settled down between peaks to the west, Levi found a small spring oozing cold water out of the ground at the foot of Harvey Peak. Twice on the way Curly stopped and stared at their back trail, but Levi could see nothing amiss either time. Still, he was edgy. The dog was usually perfectly reliable. It wasn't like him to offer a warning twice with no reason.

He was within a mile or two of the spot Luther Walters had been killed, according to Charolette. Tomorrow he'd ask her a few more questions.

He lay in his bedroll for nearly an hour before eventually falling asleep. Curly lay curled up beside him, sleeping as soundly as ever. He could hear his horse tearing grass, eating, where the seep spring had made the grass tall and lush. The moon followed the way the sun had fled, and deeper darkness settled over the land. Night birds offered a lullaby that was eventually irresistible, and he drifted off to sleep.

Near midnight Blue snorted, then squealed in fright. Curly leaped up at the same instant, growling and snarling. Levi leaped from his bedroll, gun in hand. Brush crashed and tore in an absolute bedlam of noise toward his right. It was too dark to see what it might be.

Something sailed through the air and landed on the ground fifty feet in front of him. His gun came to bear on it instantly, but it didn't move. The crashing in the brush continued. Blue continued to squeal in fright. The sounds of his hobbled flight were almost as loud as the crashing approach through the brush. The unmistakable form of a bear lumbered from the brush, heading directly toward them.

'Run, Curly!' Levi yelled. 'It's a grizzly!'

Stocking-footed, he turned and fled as fast as his legs could carry him. The sounds of the charging bear behind him gave wings to his feet. Even so, he knew it was a losing battle. No man on foot could outrun a bear. He could turn and empty his .45 into it, and it would have no effect at all, except to enrage it further. It might die tomorrow or the next day, but it wouldn't make any difference to him by then.

Out of the darkness a tall tree loomed before him. With a mighty lunge he leaped and grabbed a branch. Terror sometimes provides superhuman strength. He swung himself up, gripping the branch between his feet. He hauled himself up on to it, reached for a higher branch, and began to climb as fast as he could find branches for footholds. The tree shook violently as the bear reached and tore away the first branch he had grabbed.

He continued to climb further than he needed to. He knew a grizzly can't climb a tree. He had no idea how he knew it was a grizzly, from that fleeting glimpse in near total darkness. He was sure he was right, though. If it were a black bear instead, it would have followed him right up the tree, and he would already be getting torn to pieces in its mighty grip.

His knees suddenly turned to rubber, and he hugged the tree with both arms to keep from falling. As his breathing began to slow, he dropped a hand to his holster. The gun was there. He had no idea when he had replaced it in the holster. The last he could remember, it was in his hand.

The bear growled and tore at the base of the tree for nearly half an hour. Then it retreated to where he had camped. He listened to its sounds there for a long while, before it groused away.

Even when he was sure it was gone, he stayed where he was. Darkness was beginning to flee from the threat of dawn when at last he ventured down.

Moving silently in the dusky light before sun-up, he approached his campsite. His bedroll was torn up. All his things were strewn about. Nothing else was there.

He searched around until he recovered his boots, and gratefully put them on. He whistled sharply once. In little more than a minute Curly lunged out of the brush and ran to him. The dog crept on his belly the last yard, whimpering softly.

'Hey, fella!' Levi greeted the animal. 'You okay, boy? You stay away from him? Good dog. It's all right. He's gone. You're OK.'

Slowly the trembling animal stilled under his touch and his soothing words. When Levi rose to seek his horse, Curly's tail was out from between his legs, but it still wasn't wagging.

Daylight allowed him to follow the trail his fleeing horse had torn through the brush. He was almost sure the bear hadn't pursued it, even though grizzlies had certainly been known to do so. His chasing or killing the horse would have made enough noise; he would surely have heard it.

Half a mile away he found Blue. He was munching grass in a small clearing, as though nothing had happened out of the ordinary.

Leading him back to his campsite, Levi began the work of trying to gather as much of his gear and belongings as possible. It took an hour to find it all. What the bear hadn't eaten, he had either torn apart or mauled. The saddle had only suffered a couple deep claw scratches. One rein of his bridle had to be repaired where the bear had bitten it nearly in two.

Bear-smell all over the site made both horse and dog increasingly nervous. As soon as he could, Levi saddled up, loaded his gear, and set out.

Riding the direction from which the bear had come, he backtracked it through the trees and brush. Within less than half a mile he found horse tracks as well. He dismounted. He reached for the saddle-bag, to exchange boots for moccasins, then remembered he hadn't been able to find one of them.

Frowning, he began to follow the trail on foot. Slowly untangling the message scuffed and pressed into the ground, the picture emerged of a ridden horse dragging something, while being followed at full gallop by the bear. Just at the edge of the clearing where he had camped, the tracks of the horse veered off and fled. The bear's tracks continued straight toward his camp.

He squatted on the ground, frowning. What in the world would make a bear chase a man on horseback, then stop chasing the horseman and attack his camp instead?

The sound of something landing on the ground in the dark recurred to him. From the spot the horse changed direction, he walked a straight line to where his bedroll had been laid out. Half-way to it he found an area trampled and torn.

He knelt and felt the grass. Something odd clung to his fingers. He smelled them. Bacon!

He frowned in total confusion. His eyes widened, then narrowed as his brow pulled down in a deep scowl. A low growl, not unlike his dog's, rumbled from his throat.

'Bacon!' he muttered to his yellow dog. 'Curly, somebody drug a slab o' bacon on a rope past a grizzly to get 'im to follow, then threw it into my camp. He knew you'd wake me up, I'd jump up, and the bear would come after me sure's anything. There was someone followin' us! You told me, twice. I didn't pay

146

enough attention. He followed us till we camped. I wonder if he knew where that bear was, or just spotted him and figured it out on the spur o' the moment? Either way, it was smart. He came within a whisker o' gettin' a bear to kill me. And it woulda looked like it was plumb accidental.'

He stayed where he was until his anger was under control. When its white heat had subsided to a cold fury, he returned to his horse and set out.

CHAPTER 15

'I wonder if I could get you to back my play.'

Cap Renfro's eyes brightened. His hands gripped the cup of coffee on the table before him. He ignored his wife's sudden frown.

'Whatd'ya have in mind?'

'Well, I think I finally figured it out. I know who the killer is. But I don't have a shred of evidence. The only way I can think of, is to get him to show his hand. I think I know how to get him to come after me, so he'll have to talk to me instead of shooting me from ambush.'

'Sounds risky.'

'Yeah, I suppose it is. Well, I know it is. Maybe I'm getting old. I'd like to have you there, out of sight, to back me up.'

'Out of sight?'

'Yeah. If he sees you there, it won't work.'

'An' ya ain't gonna tell me who it is?'

'Nope. If I'm wrong, I don't want to ruin somebody's name. If I'm right, you'll figure it out when he shows up.'

'Want me to have Harm there too?'

Levi's brows lifted. 'Hadn't thought of him. Don't know why. Yeah. That'd be a good idea. Then nobody'd have to know you were even there, if things work out like they're supposed to.'

'I'd be much obliged for thet. So would the missus, wouldn't ya?' he directed toward his wife.

She appeared about to pout.

'You said you weren't going to be involved in any more gunfights and arresting people,' she protested. 'I didn't marry you to be a widow.'

'Aw, now, Pearly, I ain't gonna be in any danger. Levi's the one that'll be takin' all the risk. I'll jist be backin' 'im up, an' they won't never nobody even know I was there.'

He was still trying to console the reluctant woman as Levi rode away.

It was late afternoon when he rode down the street of Cheerful. It had taken him a long time to put the puzzle together. It had come together with a rush.

There were the tracks he searched for, leading right to a horse at the hitching rail in front of the saloon. His uncanny eye identified it instantly as the same horse he had followed so many times, only to lose the trail when it entered the road with its traffic.

There were the half-dozen hints of an unhealthy infatuation his mind had missed for much too long.

Charolette Walters had noticed it, and mentioned it the last time he talked with her. That was when it triggered.

Then he had talked with three different ranchers.

All three had been forced to fire the same hand, because of the long absences from where he was supposed to be tending cattle. He never had an explanation for where he had been, or what he had been doing.

Even so, the whole idea was so strange, so bizarre, he couldn't accept that he was right.

He dismounted beside the horse and looked around. Nobody moved on the street. Feeling like a sneak-thief, he lifted the flap of the near saddle-bag. What he sought was not there.

He walked around the horse, glanced up and down the street again, then lifted the flap of that saddle-bag. A telescope was nestled among the other things. He stifled a shout of triumph.

Quickly withdrawing the telescope, he unscrewed the end and removed the lens from the small end. He dropped both the lens and its threaded keeper into his pocket, and replaced the telescope.

As he remounted his horse, he spotted her. Ma Ferguson stood on the board sidewalk, legs spaddled, hands on her hips. She was glaring daggers at him.

'A thief as well as a gunman?' she said.

A sudden grin spread across his face.

'Now, what would make Ma Ferguson think I'm stealing something?'

'I saw you looking in that man's saddle-bag.'

'Yeah, I was. But I wasn't stealing anything. I just wanted to find out if it was true.'

'If what was true?'

'Why I'd heard that almost every cowboy in the country carried one of those tintype photographs of

Ma Ferguson in his saddle-bag. I just wanted to see if it was true.'

'What? A picture? Of me? Why I've only ever had one of those ever . . . Why that's preposterous! Why would anyone want a picture of me?'

Levi's grin was replaced with a look of serious wonder. Frowning in pretended consternation, he said:

'I guess that travelin' photography guy made a whole bunch of copies of your picture. He sells it to all the cowboys. They tell me it keeps the bears scared away from their camps.'

She stared incomprehendingly at him for a long moment, then her jaw dropped. Her eyes bulged. Her nostrils flared.

'Why, I never in my life . . .' she sputtered.

She whirled and harumphed off down the street as he mounted and rode the other direction.

When he had put his horse up at the livery barn and told Curly to stay with him, he retraced his steps to the Dusty Soul. He approached the bar near where Bucky Denton leaned on his elbows. Fred approached.

'What'll it be, Levi?'

'Nothing right now, Fred. Has Krumm been around?'

'Not today. Why?'

'Well, I think I finally got the whole thing figured out. I s'pose I oughta talk to him.'

Fred's interest quickened visibly. Levi sensed, rather than saw, Denton tense as well.

'You got the murders figured out?'

151

He kept his voice low, as though to shield it from other ears.

'Yeah, I think so. I gotta go over and talk to Myra at the store. Then I have one more thing to do, that'll sew it up tighter than a schoolmom's bloomers.'

Fred's disappointment was just as visible.

'But you ain't sayin' who done it.'

Levi shook his head.

'I can't yet. Just about there, though. If Krumm comes in, tell him I'm looking for him, will you?'

'You got it.'

Walking quickly he went outside and down the street toward the mercantile store. He pretended not to notice that Bucky Denton left the Dusty Soul and followed him at a distance.

'Levi!' Myra greeted him. 'It's about time you showed up! You haven't been in town for so long I thought you'd deserted me.'

From the corner of his eye Levi saw Bucky slip in the front door and busy himself looking through a stack of work-shirts.

'Now you know I wouldn't do that without saying goodbye. I'm afraid the day's coming, though.'

Myra's eyes clouded. 'Really? You're going to be leaving? Right away, I mean?'

'Well, I guess I'll have to. Once I get this job done, I'll have to move on to the next one. I don't suppose you'd be interested in riding out with me?'

She took a deep breath.

'Don't do that to me. We've already talked about it. I'm not interested in getting married again. We both knew you'd ride on when your job was done here. If it's meant to be, you'll be back.'

'That just might happen.'

She took another deep breath, fighting for composure.

'Anyway, you have it figured out?'

'Just about. It just hit me a while ago. I saw the answer yesterday, and didn't recognize it.'

'Now you're not making any sense.'

'Well, I finally figured out it wasn't Ben that was jealous of Lola. It was somebody else. That somebody else has been watching them, or watching Lola mostly, I suppose, with a telescope from the timber around their place. I found the tracks where he's been hanging around there a lot. I saw a lens and the thing that screws on to the end of a telescope lying on the ground, in the trees, straight south of their house yesterday. It didn't even register what it was, until I got back to town. Then it hit me. All I have to do is ride out there at first light, get it, then match it up to the telescope it fits. I know who carries that telescope in his saddle bag. I'll have him dead to rights, as soon as I go pick up that lens.'

Myra thought through everything he had said. Her eyes glistened with forbidden tears.

'Then this will probably be your last night in Cheerful?'

'Looks that way.'

She didn't even notice Bucky slip back out the door. She didn't notice anything except Levi. As soon as Bucky was gone, Levi turned his attention to her as well.

153

CHAPTER 16

It was still dark when Levi rode out of town at a brisk trot. Sun-up found him less than a mile from his destination.

He approached the site from which he was sure Bucky had last spied on the Jordan ranch. He hadn't followed him last night, to be sure he returned to his horse to see if a lens was actually missing from his telescope. He was confident he could assume that, and devoted his whole-hearted attention to Myra.

Dismounting at the edge of the timber, he dropped the reins on his horse and walked forward. He made far more noise than he was accustomed to making. He talked to his dog as he walked. He whistled a couple bars from 'Turkey In The Straw'. He pretended not to notice the faint noises trailing him.

Curly growled softly.

'I know it, Curly,' he whispered. 'Be quiet.'

Obediently the dog fell silent, but the hair along his back continued to stand.

A hundred yards into the timber Levi turned toward the clearing that surrounded the Jordans' ranch house. Muttering to himself, he said aloud: 'Let's see. It was right over here, I think. Yeah. There's the spot. There! Got it! OK! Let's head back to town, old dog. We got this one in the bag.'

He just stepped into a small space free of trees and brush when a cold voice said,

'Far enough, Hill. Let's have it.'

Turning to his right, Levi faced Bucky Denton. Denton held a rifle waist high, pointed directly at Levi's chest, finger on the trigger.

'I'll take that lens, Hill.'

Levi's eyes darted around at the circle of trees. There was no sign of either Cap Renfro or Harm Danver. He had come too early. His backing wasn't there.

'What are you talking about, Bucky?'

'Don't play dumb!' the cowboy snapped. 'I know you got it figured out.'

'Well, not quite, I don't,' Levi admitted. 'I know you've been watching Lola from here. I know you think you're in love with her. I don't know why you've been killing everyone that flirts with her, though.'

'You ain't half smart enough to understand,' Bucky retorted. 'You ain't even smart enough to do what you were supposed to do.'

'What was I supposed to do?'

'You was supposed to figure out Ben was the killer, that's what you were supposed to do! If he gets hung for all them killin's, then Miss Lola's gonna figure out that it's me she's really in love with anyway. I'll be there for 'er. I'll help her through gettin' over losin' a husband. Miss Lola, she really does love me, you know. I can tell, the way she looks at me. I can tell, the way she smiles at me sometimes. She jist can't show it none, so long's Ben's there. She already suspects maybe Ben's the one doin' the killin', too. That's makin' her love me even more. Jist as soon as he's outa the way, everything's gonna work out jist right.'

'You really are in love with her, aren't you?'

'O' course I'm in love with her! I proved it, too. I proved it every time one o' them guys got too friendly. It ain't fittin', them flirtin' around with Miss Lola like that. They had it comin'. Ever' one of 'em.'

'You know you can't get away with it, don't you, Bucky.'

'Why can't I? I got away with it this long. That ain't all I got figgered out, neither.'

'Really? What else do you have figured out?'

'You're the one gonna get rid o' Ben for me after all.'

'How do you figure that?'

'See this gun I got. This rifle? It ain't mine. It's Ben's rifle. I done slipped in an' stole it last night. Ya see, I got them dogs all likin' me, cause I been bringin' 'em meat scraps a long time. They don't even bark when I slip up around the place. That's how come I know it's really me that Miss Lola loves, 'steada Ben. You know what? She don't love Ben atall. They don't even never do nothin'. In bed, I mean. I kin slip up an' watch in the windows any time I want to, so I know. I went an' took Ben's rifle last night. Then I tol' the marshal that you was hanging around out here in the trees spyin' on them, an' Ben found

156

out, an' Ben was fixin' to shoot you fer it. So now all I gotta do is shoot ya with Ben's rifle, drop it here on the ground, an' the marshal will find it and you both in another hour or so. Now give me the lens outa my telescope. Where's it at?'

Levi's mind raced. He went for the only chance he had.

'Take 'im, Curly!' he said.

Instantly the dog streaked forward. His lips rolled back from his teeth. A low growl rumbled from his throat. He crossed the distance between Levi and Denton with blurring speed.

Bucky's eyes flickered from Levi to the charging dog. The rifle barrel wavered.

Levi's forty-five leaped into his hand, spouting fire. At the same instant, two rifles barked from the edge of the trees.

Curly leaped, fastening his teeth into the arm that held a rifle pointed at his master. By the time he reached the ground with that arm firmly gripped in his mouth, he realized there was no resistance. It belonged to a dead man.

Cap Renfro and Harm Danver stepped from the trees. Levi thumbed out the spent brass and reloaded his pistol, then dropped it into its holster.

'I didn't hear you boys at all,' he said. 'I thought I must've gotten here too early.'

Cap grinned. 'Been here since jist after midnight. Didn't wanta take no chances. Didn't wanta tip our hand, though, till Harm heard enough to hang the boy. We was jist fixin' to call out to 'im to throw up his hands, when you sicced yer dog on 'im. Thet was a neat play. Guess ya didn't need us after all.'

'This whole thing was a pretty big gamble anyway,' Harm put in. 'That boy was crazy enough to just shoot you before he even said anything.'

Levi considered it, and didn't like the feeling it left in his gut.

'Yeah,' was all he could think to say. 'I'll have to be more careful next time.'

But in his heart he knew he probably wouldn't.